The Sisters

by Richard Alfieri

A SAMUEL FRENCH ACTING EDITION

SAMUEL FRENCH

FOUNDED 1830

NEW YORK HOLLYWOOD LONDON TORONTO

SAMUELFRENCH.COM

MUSIC USE NOTE

Licensees are solely responsible for obtaining formal written permission from copyright owners to use copyrighted music in the performance of this play and are strongly cautioned to do so. If no such permission is obtained by the licensee, then the licensee must use only original music that the licensee owns and controls. Licensees are solely responsible and liable for all music clearances and shall indemnify the copyright owners of the play and their licensing agent, Samuel French, Inc., against any costs, expenses, losses and liabilities arising from the use of music by licensees.

IMPORTANT BILLING AND CREDIT
REQUIREMENTS

All producers of *THE SISTERS* *must* give credit to the Author of the Play in all programs distributed in connection with performances of the Play, and in all instances in which the title of the Play appears for the purposes of advertising, publicizing or otherwise exploiting the Play and/or a production. The name of the Author *must* appear on a separate line on which no other name appears, immediately following the title and *must* appear in size of type not less than fifty percent of the size of the title type.

THE SISTERS was first produced at the Pasadena Playhouse in Pasadena, California on July 16, 1995. The performance was directed by Arthur Allan Seidelman, with sets by Gary Wissman, costumes by Dawna Oak, lighting by Kevin Mahan, sound by Frederick W. Boot. The Production Stage Manager was Tami Toon. The cast was as follows:

GARY SOKOL . . . . Paul Regina

DR. CHERBIN . . . . Pat Corley

DAVID TURZIN . . . . Matthew Letscher

MARCIA PRIOR GLASS . . . . Meg Foster

OLGA PRIOR . . . . Season Hubley

VINCENT ANTONELLI . . . . Tony Musante

ANDREW PRIOR . . . . Craig Wasson

NANCY PECKET . . . . Tammy Lauren

IRENE PRIOR . . . . Charlotte Ross

HARRY GLASS . . . . Alan Feinstein

NURSE . . . . Pamela Sam

PARAMEDIC ONE . . . . Ty Biggs

PARAMEDIC TWO . . . . Bill Ritter

CHARACTERS

GARY SOKOL
DR. CHEBRIN
DAVID TURZIN
MARCIA PRIOR GLASS
OLGA PRIOR
VINCENT ANTONELLI
ANDREW PRIOR
NANCY PECKET
IRENE PRIOR
HARRY GLASS
NURSE
PARAMEDIC ONE
PARAMEDIC TWO

SETTING

ACT I
Scene 1: The faculty lounge of Manhattan Crest College on the Upper East Side of New York City. Late afternoon.

Scene 2: The same. Two hours later.

Scene 3: A hospital room and waiting area. Later that evening.

ACT II
The faculty lounge. Four months later.

To my parents
Etelvina and Sam Alfieri

ACT I

Scene 1

(As house lights dim, piano music, the haunting strains of Schumann's "Of Foreign Lands and People," rises, then:)

(Curtain rises on the faculty lounge of Manhattan Crest College on the Upper East Side of New York City. The split-level room is large and lavishly designed, betraying the building's original purpose as a sumptuous private residence. Twin staircases lead down from each end of an upstage balustraded mezzanine to the main room downstage. A large mahogany conference table and chairs dominate the mezzanine. In the main room below, an overstuffed leather chair faces a fireplace right, a baby-grand piano stands beside the left wall, and an elongated upholstered seat emerges from the wainscoting between the twin staircases. Mahogany tables and floor lamps with period shades complete the club-room decor.)

(On the mezzanine level, there is an interior door upstage left and an exterior glass-and-wrought-iron door upstage right, which opens onto a small terrace with steps leading down to a portion of flagstone courtyard below right. On the upstage wall above the conference table, a wide three-paneled bay window faces onto the courtyard. Through the window, late-afternoon sunlight illuminates the foliage of summer, and stately Georgian buildings are visible on the opposite perimeter.)

(Portraits of former college presidents line the walls of both rooms and gaze upon the scene like a collective superconscious. Prominent among these portraits is that

of August Prior, the father of the three sisters. The artist caught his stern, handsome face in a half-smile that seems designed to draw the viewer forward – not to welcome, but to assess.)

(Three faculty members are on stage as the scene opens. **DR. CHEBRIN***, sixties, wearing a well-worn blazer with college insignia, sits reading the newspaper by the fireplace in the main room. He seems quite oblivious to the activities of the two younger professors engaged in a rather vocal game of chess at one corner of the conference table above.* **DAVID TURZIN** *is a thirty year-old philosophy professor; he stares at the board and patiently endures the rantings of his slightly older opponent,* **GARY SOKOL***, a political science professor. Piano music fades as:)*

DR. CHEBRIN. *(reading aloud to no one in particular)* Ah! Three people killed by a gunman in a subway car in Queens! We're like rats in a maze – scurrying around, devouring each other.

DAVID. Doctor, did you buy another paper with only bad news in it?

SOKOL. Jesus, would you shut up! What are you talking to him for? Concentrate on your next move.

DR. CHEBRIN. Ah! A Bronx cabbie was robbed and strangled with a G-string by two twin sisters who were topless dancers!

DAVID. If they were twins, there could only have been two of them, Doctor.

SOKOL. Move already! God, it's like playing with statuary! I'm imposing a two-minute time limit...

(checks his watch)

...starting...now!

DAVID. No time limit. We agreed.

SOKOL. You didn't tell me you suffered from A.D.D.!

(**MARCIA PRIOR**, *a beautiful woman in her early thirties, tastefully dressed, rushes into the courtyard right carrying packages and a shopping bag. As she ascends the steps to the terrace, she calls behind:*)

MARCIA. Hurry, Olga...!

(**OLGA PRIOR**, *also burdened with packages, enters a few steps behind her sister. She is an attractive but severe-looking thirty-five, wearing a skirt suit befitting a professor. As she climbs the steps behind* **MARCIA***:*)

OLGA. Honestly, Marcia, I can't have my students see me bolting about campus like a hyperactive Clydesdale.

DR. CHEBRIN. Ah! A woman in the Bronx was locked in a closet for three days for starching her husband's boxer shorts!

DAVID. *(turns to* **DOCTOR** *suspiciously)* You made that one up.

SOKOL. *(snapping his fingers impatiently)* Hey!

DR. CHEBRIN. It's right here, David. *(shaking his head)* It's a violent world out there.

(**MARCIA** *bursts in from upstage right door and unceremoniously deposits a box on the conference table. The young professors look up, astonished, as* **OLGA** *enters behind her.*)

MARCIA. Good evening, gentlemen.

DAVID. Hello, Marcia...Olga.

OLGA. David...Gary.

SOKOL. Oh great, another distraction.

MARCIA. Thank you, Mr. Sokol, it's always lovely to see you, too.

(**MARCIA** *makes her way down the right staircase with the rest of her packages.*)

MARCIA. *(smiling)* Dr. Chebrin. You came.

(**DR. CHEBRIN** *lowers his newspaper and beams when he sees* **MARCIA***.*)

DR. CHEBRIN. Dear Marcia. Of course. All I have to do evenings is grow older and read my newspaper.

SOKOL. And follow homicide detectives around town for late-breaking atrocities.

OLGA. *(removing cake from box on table)* What a beautiful cake, Marcia!

DAVID. Is Irene coming soon?

OLGA. She has a class until six.

> *(checks her watch)*

My God, Marcia, not a moment to spare!

MARCIA. *(rushing up the stairs)* I told you we should have started sooner.

> *(to DAVID and SOKOL as she removes decorations from bag)*

Gentlemen, we're pressed for time.

> *(She sweeps the chess pieces into the bag and removes the board.)*

Checkmate.

> *(SOKOL and DAVID cry out in protest as MARCIA, undeterred, hands them decorations. DR. CHEBRIN, SOKOL, and DAVID assist MARCIA in tacking streamers to the walls and placing party items about the room as the scene progresses.)*

OLGA. I've been behind schedule since my lecture class this morning. The question and answer was interminable.

DR. CHEBRIN. They were trying to fathom your profundities.

OLGA. Please. The girls were all mentally filing their nails and the boys were deciding who in class is the worthiest recipient of their next erection.

> *(MARCIA laughs.)*

No one listens anymore.

DAVID. That's hard to believe. There's a long wait list to get into any of your classes.

MARCIA. Oh, Olga knows that. It's just a ploy for reassurance.

(**OLGA** *stops and stares at* **MARCIA**; *a line has been crossed.*)

OLGA. I don't think being married to a psychologist qualifies you to practice on unwilling patients – and in public.

MARCIA. I'm your sister and these are our friends. Don't be so sensitive.

(checks her watch)

Where is Harry, anyway? And Andrew?

OLGA. Changing the subject after saying something cruel and *insensitive* is a tactic Marcia learned as a child and never quite outgrew.

(off **MARCIA**'*s stony stare)*

I'm your sister and these are our friends.

MARCIA. Let's hurry up with this. She'll be here before we're set up and ruin the surprise.

SOKOL. You give her a surprise party every year. Do you think she's not expecting it? And would you want her not to? It would mean a serious flaw in her reasoning powers.

MARCIA. We told her we didn't have time to arrange a party this year. If she believed us that's not stupidity, Mr Sokol, it's suspension of disbelief.

SOKOL. Suspension of disbelief is a literary device. When employed in life it's called *psychosis*.

(There is a tentative knock at the upstage left door. Everyone freezes.)

OLGA. Oh my God, there she is.

DAVID. Why would she knock?

SOKOL. She wants to make sure we're ready to surprise her.

MARCIA. Damn, and half of us aren't here. Let's yell loud to compensate.

(lifting her voice)

Come in!

(As the door opens everyone in the room yells a deafening "SURPRISE!" **VINCENT ANTONELLI**, *a robust-looking man in his mid-forties, corporately dressed, stands stunned in the doorway with a tentative smile on his face.)*

SOKOL. Oh look! She surprised us back by coming in drag! Irene, you card.

VINCENT. Do I have the right room? I'm looking for the Prior sisters.

OLGA. We're the Prior sisters. At least, two of them.

VINCENT. I'm Vincent Antonelli.

*(***MARCIA*** and ***OLGA*** share a blank look.)*

I was your father's teaching assistant in Charleston.

OLGA. *(crossing to him)* I remember. Just before he came to New York to accept the chancellorship. I'm –

VINCENT. Don't tell me...Olga. The serious one.

OLGA. That's right.

VINCENT. I remember you all as girls –

SOKOL. Good memory.

*(***VINCENT*** takes ***OLGA***'s hand, bows slightly, and kisses it.)*

VINCENT. It's a pleasure to renew your acquaintance.

OLGA. Likewise, Vincent.

*(turning to ***MARCIA***)*

Do you remember my sister –

VINCENT. Don't tell me....

*(stares at ***MARCIA*** for a moment)*

Marcia. You were the...

*(He hesitates, with an awkward glance at ***OLGA***.)*

OLGA. The beautiful one. You can say it.

(with a tinge of sarcasm)

She's my sister and these are our friends.

VINCENT. *(to MARCIA)* And you're still beautiful.

MARCIA. *(somewhat embarrassed – and intrigued)* Thank you. And welcome...

*(As **MARCIA** crosses toward the left staircase to greet **VINCENT**, he begins crossing down to her.)*

VINCENT. No, please. Let me come to you.

SOKOL. *(to DAVID and DR. CHEBRIN)* This guy's like a day in Finishing School.

DR. CHEBRIN. *(to DAVID and SOKOL)* It's that Southern thing – if they're not kissing your hand they're lynching you.

*(**MARCIA** and **VINCENT** meet on the staircase. He takes her hand and kisses it.)*

MARCIA. I remember you now. You were in love with that hysterical girl who was always praying.

VINCENT. Yes. Helen. I married her.

MARCIA. I'm so sorry.

(then, quickly)

I mean, not that you married her. But for my rude...

SOKOL. *(to DAVID and DR. CHEBRIN)* It's terrible to see charm floundering like this. Like watching a cat lose its balance and fall in the toilet.

VINCENT. Please don't mention it. That was years ago.

MARCIA. We all said that about Helen because we had crushes on you...

SOKOL. *(to DAVID and DR. CHEBRIN)* Countering her insult with a clumsy compliment.

MARCIA. *(chagrinned)* I mean, we didn't *all* say it...Oh my.

VINCENT. *(good-naturedly)* We have two lovely little girls now, and I adore them.

MARCIA. I'm so glad.

(leading him into the main room)

Please meet our friends and faculty members. Dr. Chebrin, the head of the English department.

VINCENT. It's a pleasure, Doctor.

DR. CHEBRIN. Don't call me Doctor. I can't cure anything.

MARCIA. David Turzin, professor of philosophy.

VINCENT. *(shaking hands)* Oh...philosophy.

DAVID. Is that an expression of approval or disapproval?

MARCIA. David's a bit defensive about the subject.

DAVID. In a materialistic society questions of ethics and logic are considered luxuries no one can afford.

VINCENT. Ethics and logic are necessities, not luxuries, in my line of work.

MARCIA. What is your line of work, Mr. Antonelli?

VINCENT. Vincent, please. I work for an image-consulting firm.

SOKOL. Image consultant. David, you finally met someone with a job more expendable than your own.

(**VINCENT** *laughs.*)

MARCIA. Vincent, this boorish man is Gary Sokol, political science professor.

(As **VINCENT** *shakes* **SOKOL**'s *hand:*)

Mr. Sokol prides himself on being completely candid – and irritating.

VINCENT. Those are just external mannerisms. Our true character lies within, I believe, beyond our cognitive powers.

SOKOL. If you can't perceive it, it's not there.

MARCIA. In your case, I'm sure that's true, Gary.

VINCENT. *(referring to decorations)* Am I interrupting a private party?

MARCIA. You're not interrupting at all. You must stay and be our guest.

OLGA. It's a surprise birthday party for our sister Irene.

VINCENT. Irene – the baby.

MARCIA. Still the baby, yes, even at twenty-two.

(**ANDREW PRIOR** *rushes up the terrace steps and enters the mezzanine through the upstage right door. He is*

thirty, pleasant-looking, on the soft side, casually dressed.
He anxiously scans the room.)

ANDREW. Is Nancy here yet?

OLGA. No, and neither is Irene.

(pointedly)

It's Irene's party, you know.

MARCIA. Andrew, come meet Vincent Antonelli – from Charleston.

*(As **ANDREW** starts down the right staircase:)*

DR. CHEBRIN. *(to **DAVID** and **SOKOL**)* Charleston – the magic word that brings people down that staircase.

MARCIA. He was Father's teaching assistant. Don't you remember?

ANDREW. I, uh...

*(As **VINCENT** shakes **ANDREW**'s hand:)*

VINCENT. Of course you don't. I was much older. You were just a boy. I remember you were always called...

*(**VINCENT** seems suddenly at a loss.)*

ANDREW. The brother. In a house full of sisters that was my only term of distinction.

SOKOL. *(to **DAVID** and **DR. CHEBRIN**)* The serious one, the baby, the brother, and the *beautiful* one. I'd say Marcia lucked out when they were assigning nicknames in Charleston.

ANDREW. *(to **VINCENT**)* Welcome.

*(to **CHEBRIN, DAVID, SOKOL**)*

Gentlemen.

*(**DR. CHEBRIN, DAVID,** and **SOKOL** greet Andrew.)*

MARCIA. We were just convincing Vincent to stay for Irene's party.

VINCENT. *(checks his watch)* I really just stopped by to say hello, since I'm in town on business.

ANDREW. Irene would love to meet anyone from Charleston
– the mythical city.

OLGA. That's true. She's heard all the stories, but was too
young to remember anything.

VINCENT. She's never been back?

MARCIA. No. We still own the house on King Street, but
we've been renting it out for years. As soon as the current lease is up we're going to go back and make a
home of it again. Back to a simpler life. Do you still
live there?

VINCENT. Not for years. My company's based in Baltimore.

DR. CHEBRIN. Is that where you lost your regional accent?

VINCENT. I'm second generation Italian, Doctor. Just
enough time to lose the old country accent; not
enough time to acquire a Southern one.

SOKOL. That difficult transition from immigrant to red-
neck.

VINCENT. Mr. Sokol, I appreciate your humor and look forward to discovering your *other* positive qualities.

DR. CHEBRIN. Don't hold your breath.

SOKOL. *(to VINCENT)* That was pretty vicious coming from
an image consultant.

(**NANCY PECKET** *runs up the terrace steps and bursts
into the mezzanine through the upstage right door. She
is a very pretty young woman in her early twenties with
obvious make-up and a thick mane of hair. She wears a
"party" dress that is a little too short, too tight, and too
shiny. She begins talking before getting her bearings.*)

NANCY. *(breathless)* Am I late? Is she here yet? Where's
Andrew?

SOKOL. Yes. No. Down here.

(**ANDREW** *bounds up the stairs to* **NANCY**.)

ANDREW. Hi, babe.

NANCY. Hi, babe.

*(ANDREW *gives* NANCY *an intimate kiss. They grope for a moment before* ANDREW *draws her to the balustrade to present her to the group.* OLGA *and* MARCIA *wear strained smiles in* NANCY*'s presence.)*

ANDREW. Nance, I think you know everyone.

NANCY. Hi all around.

SOKOL. Hi right back at you.

ANDREW. And this is Vincent Antonelli from Charleston.

(proudly to VINCENT*)*

This is Nancy Pecket, my fiancé.

*(OLGA *flinches visibly at the word.* MARCIA *seems to develop a sudden headache.)*

VINCENT. I'm pleased to meet you.

NANCY. Likewise. Where's Irene? Where's Harry?

MARCIA. Harry's probably with a particularly crazy patient who's having either a breakdown or a breakthrough –someone who just realized his father's a bastard and his mother's a bitch and is either elated or crestfallen by the discovery.

VINCENT. What?

OLGA. Her husband's a psychologist.

MARCIA. *(to* NANCY*)* Irene has a class until six.

NANCY. *(checking her watch)* It's six now!

MARCIA. They're not beaming her over. It'll take her a few minutes to walk here.

OLGA. Still, the candles aren't even on the cake yet. Andrew, help me.

NANCY. I'll help.

*(NANCY *begins assisting* OLGA *in the mezzanine.* MARCIA *remains in the main room below.)*

VINCENT. Irene's a student here?

MARCIA. Graduates this spring.

(indicating her father's portrait)

We're all drawn here like moths to Father's big flame.

(**OLGA** *gives* **MARCIA** *a disapproving look, which*
MARCIA *either does not notice or ignores.*)

MARCIA. *(cont'd)* Irene's an English major. Olga teaches
English Lit. I met Harry here when he was taking one
day a week from his practice to give a lecture course on
Jung – a bunch of bullshit, really, but I was too young
to realize it at the time. And Andrew was a graduate
student in music and is now an associate professor.
That's how he met Nancy.

NANCY. Extension course. I wasn't a full-time student.

MARCIA. Nancy thinks that takes the onus off screwing the
professor.

NANCY. *(aghast)* I...

MARCIA. Just kidding. You were both adults. Who cares?
That's how I met Harry, rue the day.

ANDREW. It's not what you say, Marcia, it's how you say it.

MARCIA. Oh, it's not my content, but my form? Maybe Mr.
Antonelli can help me polish up my social presenta-
tion. Start with me and work his way up to Mr. Sokol.

SOKOL. *(to* **MARCIA***)* I think you're the far greater challenge
this evening.

ANDREW. It's not your form or your content that disturb
me, Marcia – it's your *intention.*

MARCIA. *(innocently)* My intention is merely informational.
I was explaining that, as a clerk at Bergdorf's, Nancy
heard the call and was mesmerized. "I'm a shopgirl,"
she said, "with no time for a degree, but I can take an
extension course at night – "

OLGA. *(apprehensive)* Marcia...

ANDREW. *(warning)* Marcia...

NANCY. I can tell my own story, you know. It's *my* story.

MARCIA. Oh, I think I can tell it much more interestingly
with my objective distance. That's what a good biogra-
pher is for.

SOKOL. *(to* **DR. CHEBRIN** *and* **DAVID***)* She used me as a tem-
porary diversion to get herself off the hot seat, then
she lifted her dress and put her ass right back on it.

DR. CHEBRIN. *(trying to avoid a disaster, gently)* Marcia, why not let Nancy tell it.

MARCIA. Well, I'll tell my version first and you see if it isn't better. So, after a long day of selling black pantyhose to middle-aged Upper-East-Side women obsessed with cellulite and varicose veins, Nancy was drawn to Manhattan Crest College like Trilby to Svengali, like Tsarina Alexandra to Rasputin. A voice in her head kept repeating, "You don't have the patience to get a degree, but why not take an extension course instead? Wow all the other clerks with your knowledge of great music. Smugly identify all the Mantovani tunes as they come over the Muzak."

ANDREW. How obnoxious! Really, Marcia, I don't know what's come over you lately.

MARCIA. Oh, where's your sense of humor? Nancy sees the fun in all this.

SOKOL. Yeah. Not since her head-on collision has she had such a great time.

NANCY. No, I don't, Marcia. Really, I don't.

MARCIA. I'm sorry. Then you tell your version. Or, better yet, you can tell the story of how I met Harry to get back at me.

ANDREW. Oh, stop now.

> *(**ANDREW** draws back, then stops, noticing that **NANCY** has not moved. She seems to be considering the challenge.)*

SOKOL. The invitation didn't say anything about psycho-drama.

NANCY. You really want me to tell it?

MARCIA. *(as if to a child)* Do-you-know-it?

NANCY. *(almost sweetly)* I think so.

MARCIA. Then tell it.

OLGA. Oh, enough.

VINCENT. Perhaps I should leave. I feel somehow responsible.

MARCIA. Don't be ridiculous. You're as incidental as the spectator at an ancient Greek tragedy. The play is really an offering to the gods, not the audience.

(to NANCY)

Go ahead, Nancy, make your little offering.

(NANCY *steps to the balustrade.)*

NANCY. Let's see...

MARCIA. Terrible start. Just launch right into the narrative.

NANCY. Alright. You were a lonely woman in her late twenties who had just had an unhappy love affair – your *latest* – that left you suicidal – *again.*

MARCIA. I like that use of the unflattering modifier for emphasis. Very effective.

NANCY. Thank you. And nobody could convince you to go into therapy, but you agreed to attend some psychology lectures instead –

MARCIA. *(to* VINCENT) It's true. We're a family of scholars.

NANCY. And you met Harry, who was attracted to you because you were so *fucked-up.*

ANDREW. Stop this.

OLGA. Yes.

MARCIA. No. It's true. I *was* fucked-up. A walking textbook. Harry looked right past my physical attributes to what really got him hot – a damaged psyche.

(to NANCY)

So go on.

NANCY. So he thought he could make you happy, so he married you, but instead of making you happy you've made him miserable and depressed. And you won't have any children –

ANDREW. This is horrible and primitive, stop it now!

MARCIA. No, Andrew. You've given Nancy your balls, now let her use them.

SOKOL. *(fascinated)* This is a *major* offering to the gods. They'll be belching and farting this one for days.

NANCY. You won't have any children because you're too selfish, and unstable, and you might hurt them emotionally – or *physically*.

(**MARCIA** *is stunned for a moment, then composes herself.*)

MARCIA. There. I think Nancy topped me with that story, don't you, gentlemen?

SOKOL. Definitely.

MARCIA. More probing, more vicious. Although almost completely lacking in humor. And I think even Nancy would have to admit she borrowed some of the three and four-syllable words from Andrew. A regurgitation of his family ruminations, but a creditable one which Nancy managed to imbue with her own direct style. Brava!

(**MARCIA** *extends her hand up to the balustrade for* **NANCY** *to shake.* **NANCY** *hesitates a moment, reaches down tentatively, then stops.*)

MARCIA. Come on. I'm not going to pull you down. The fall wouldn't kill you, just get you a lot more sympathy from Andrew.... Come on.

(**NANCY** *reaches down again, but before their hands can touch,* **OLGA** *cries out:*)

OLGA. (*looking through the bay window*) Oh my God, here she comes. Quickly, help me light the candles.

(**ANDREW** *helps* **OLGA** *light the candles.* **NANCY** *and* **MARCIA** *turn away from each other without clasping hands.*)

(**IRENE** *crosses up the terrace steps and enters through the upstage right door. She is a pretty, fresh-faced twenty-two year old, simply dressed, carrying a book bag. She is delighted to see the room full of people and laughs gleefully when they yell "Surprise!" almost in unison.*)

(**IRENE'**s *reactions to situations throughout the scene are slightly exaggerated, but, given the circumstances, this goes virtually unnoticed by the others.*)

IRENE. Oh... you all! I had a feeling!

SOKOL. Call it a crazy hunch.

(MARCIA, OLGA, and ANDREW rush to embrace IRENE.)

MARCIA. Happy birthday, darling.

ANDREW. Happy Birthday!

OLGA. Sweet thing.

(As OLGA finishes lighting the candles, guests on the lower level make their way up to the mezzanine and gather around the table.)

IRENE. Oh, Nancy!

NANCY. Happy birthday, Irene.

IRENE. Thank you.... Doctor Chebrin!

DR. CHEBRIN. Many happy returns, darling.

IRENE. Oh, thank you. Thank you for being here.... David!

DAVID. Happy birthday, Irene.

(DAVID embraces IRENE and gives her an awkward and prolonged kiss which embarrasses IRENE and raises eyebrows among the guests.)

SOKOL. Gee, David, why not use Irene's birthday as an excuse to explore her digestive tract with your tongue.

(DAVID turns suddenly and angrily on SOKOL.)

DAVID. Why don't you just shut up, Gary! You're really rude and offensive, you know that?

SOKOL. *(surprised at the outburst)* Of course. You just noticed?

IRENE. Please, David, he was just kidding.

MARCIA. *(to IRENE)* Don't worry. It's been like this all evening. Must be planetary.

(drawing VINCENT forward)

Irene, this is Vincent Antonelli – from Charleston.

DR. CHEBRIN. Charleston! So much for getting a piece of cake any time soon.

IRENE. *(taking VINCENT's hand)* Oh my. It's a pleasure.

SOKOL. *(before VINCENT can speak)* The pleasure is always his.

VINCENT. Thank you, Mr. Sokol.

MARCIA. Vincent was Father's teaching aid in Charleston. He knew us as girls.

IRENE. Really!

MARCIA. Yes, and Nancy and I helped fill him in on some of our *recent* family history.

OLGA. *(quickly)* Okay! All lit! Make a wish!

(IRENE stands before the cake and stares, transfixed, at the circle of light.)

IRENE. Just being here with you all –

SOKOL. No. Make a good wish – something involving major appliances or real estate.

IRENE. Wait. I've got it.

(IRENE takes a deep breath and blows out the candles. Everyone cheers and claps.)

ALL. Speech!

IRENE. Okay, okay! ...I know I'll always be the baby in the family, but I'm not a baby anymore. Father said something to me when we were still in Charleston....

(MARCIA and OLGA exchange a conspiratorial look.)

He said your most precious possessions are your family. They are the supporting beam of your life, the light that guides you, the sacred bosom that –

SOKOL. Three metaphors and you're out.

DAVID. *(angrily)* Would you just –

IRENE. No, Gary's right. This is so corny. I just want to say I love you all, and even though I know you'll always be there to support me –

SOKOL. Like a beam.

IRENE. *(smiling)* Right, Gary, like a beam – I want very much to be strong enough to support myself and you, if you need me. That's my goal for twenty-two.

(shrugs)

That's all.

(**OLGA** *and* **MARCIA** *kiss* **IRENE.**)

MARCIA. That was lovely, darling.

SOKOL. I feel like I was just hit with a stack of Hallmark cards.

DAVID. *(disgusted by* **SOKOL***)* Brother.

IRENE. Gary's right. Let's eat.

OLGA. I'll cut the cake.

ANDREW. Marcia, could I speak to you for a moment?

MARCIA. Sure. Shoot.

ANDREW. Downstairs, please.

SOKOL. Uh-oh.

MARCIA. Everyone knows you're pissed off, so why not be open about it and get it over with.

OLGA. Oh, please, not now.

IRENE. What happened?

OLGA. Nothing.

ANDREW. *(angrily to* **MARCIA***)* Everyone knows I'm pissed off, but they don't know exactly how pissed off I am, or how I'm going to express it! I'd like to share those details with you alone.

(**MARCIA** *stares at* **ANDREW** *for a moment, then walks down the stairs. He follows.* **IRENE** *looks after them in bewilderment;* **OLGA** *tries to distract her.*)

OLGA. *(handing cut cake to* **IRENE***)* Here, darling, help me pass these around. Maybe you'll play the piano for us later.

IRENE. Sure....

(**OLGA** *keeps the party going upstairs as* **ANDREW** *and* **MARCIA** *speak downstage.*)

MARCIA. I know what you're going to say, but you know I can't stand that vulgar girl and you insist on foisting her upon your sisters and me. I can no longer disguise my true feelings about her –

ANDREW. You won't even give me the satisfaction of chewing you out! What are you chastising me for? You should be apologizing. You attack her and embarrass her with your vicious humor –

MARCIA. I ran out of charm with her a long time ago.

ANDREW. You ran out of everything, Marcia – including basic human decency. You impugn my masculinity in front of everyone!

MARCIA. Wait till she finishes with you, Andrew. I don't want to hurt you, I want to *warn* you. You see her as a girl, but I know the kind of woman she is. I know what she's capable of doing to a man.

ANDREW. You *should* know. You've been doing it to your husband for five years.

MARCIA. Perhaps. Call me a bitch, a shrew, a harpy. *That* one *(indicates* **NANCY***)* could give me lessons.

(At that moment, **HARRY** *enters through the upstage left interior door.* **HARRY** *is in his late thirties, dressed in suit and tie.)*

HARRY. Am I terribly late?

SOKOL. You certainly missed all the juicy stuff.

HARRY. *(crossing to* **IRENE***)* I'm so sorry. Happy birthday, Irene.

IRENE. Thank you. Relax, Harry. Have a piece of cake.

HARRY. *(looking around)* Where's...?

(spots **MARCIA***)*

Oh.

*(***HARRY** *crosses down the left staircase to greet* **MARCIA***.)*

MARCIA. *(rushed, quietly to* **ANDREW***)* I'm sorry, Andrew. I'll be better. I'm sorry. Don't hate me.

*(***MARCIA** *kisses* **ANDREW***, who responds grudgingly, as* **HARRY** *approaches.)*

HARRY. Am I interrupting something?

ANDREW. No. Not at all, Harry. Let's join the others, shall we?

MARCIA. I'll be up in a minute.

(ANDREW *nods and crosses up the stairs.*)

(HARRY *crosses to* MARCIA *and kisses her perfunctorily on the cheek.*)

HARRY. Sorry I'm late.

MARCIA. I know. I heard.

HARRY. Jesus, Marcia, I had a patient.

MARCIA. I've heard that, too.

HARRY. *(checks his watch)* How late is this going to go?

MARCIA. You just got here!

HARRY. We have the Waldmann soiree this evening.

MARCIA. We have no such thing.

HARRY. I told you about it. You said yes.

MARCIA. How could I have said yes? It's my sister's birthday.

HARRY. You said yes, we'd stop by later.

MARCIA. Never!

HARRY. Maybe you're blocking it because you don't want to go.

MARCIA. Maybe I blocked it, repressed it, denied it, and sublimated it, but I'll guarantee you this – I am not going to spend the evening with those two ossified old farts.

HARRY. They head the foundation, and the foundation supplies most of my referrals. Or did you think my patients just walk in off the street when they're feeling a little crazy?

MARCIA. I don't care if they're airlifted from Bellevue, I'm not going.

HARRY. You take no responsibility for maintaining my career, which maintains your lifestyle.

MARCIA. Which maintains your career! What would you do without a well-dressed wife to display to that group of overeducated dullards and closet loonies you call your colleagues. It's symbiosis, Harry. But, here...

(**MARCIA** *removes her earrings, necklace, bracelet, and rings. Guests in the mezzanine stop their conversations and turn to stare at* **MARCIA** *and* **HARRY**.)

MARCIA. *(cont'd)* Let's break the cycle. You take the ornamentation,

(handing her jewels to **HARRY**)

I'll take the evening off.

HARRY. *(with a glance toward the mezzanine)* You love these little spectacles, don't you? They validate you somehow.

MARCIA. And you, too – the good and caring doctor with the mad wife. Patiently enduring me like an ongoing homework assignment.

HARRY. Your state of mind is nothing for me to be proud of; it's a professional liability – and so are you!

MARCIA. As usual, you made it from pompous to obnoxious without stopping at amusing.

HARRY. *(placing the jewels back in Marcia's hand)* Keep those. You lose all your charm without them.

(**MARCIA** *angrily throws the jewels across the room.* **HARRY** *turns, crosses up the left staircase, and exits through the upstage left door.)*

OLGA. *(whispering)* Maybe you should play now, dear.

(**IRENE** *drifts to the piano and begins softly playing Beethoven's "Für Elise.")*

(**MARCIA** *stands quietly for a moment. Conversation has stopped completely upstairs; everyone looks at* **MARCIA**. *She turns away from them and faces downstage.)*

MARCIA. *(quietly)* Well, this is no fun. Let's open the presents.

(Piano music continues as curtain falls.)

Scene 2

(Piano music continues as curtain rises on faculty lounge. Two hours later. Night.)

*(****MARCIA*** *and* ***VINCENT*** *are alone, dismantling the last of the decorations and clearing the party remnants. Several of the lights have been shut, creating a mood somewhere between romantic and eerie.)*

(Music fades as:)

MARCIA. You really didn't have to do this.

VINCENT. I wouldn't have considered leaving you alone.

MARCIA. It's nothing new to me, believe me. But, won't your wife be concerned about you?

VINCENT. My wife's in Baltimore.

MARCIA. Oh.... Excuse me. That was shamelessly coy and indirect of me.

VINCENT. But the answer to your question is "no," she wouldn't be too concerned.

MARCIA. It's none of my business, really. Bearing my emotional scars in public is a distasteful habit I've acquired; I have no right to ask you or anyone else to do the same.

VINCENT. Why not? It's really just a search for some kindredness and consolation, isn't it? What a desolate sadness to think that you're the only person who suffers in marriage. My marriage is an abysmal failure, a barely-manageable disaster.

MARCIA. But why stay – ?

VINCENT. Why stay in it? You barter away so many pieces of yourself in a long relationship, I'm not sure I remember which are mine or how I would go about reclaiming them.

*(****MARCIA*** *nods.)*

And then there are my girls. They're the light of my life, and I couldn't bear to lose them. But I'm sure your father felt the same way about you girls.

MARCIA. Exactly. Wanted us with him all the time. Every goddamn minute – for eternity, really. Father's voice echoing in our heads, *(turning to the portrait)* his portraits and photographs plastered on our walls. Father marching through time with us, his presence...*indelible.*

VINCENT. I had no idea you –

MARCIA. Hated him a little bit? It's natural for a child to resist authority, don't you think? And Father was the ultimate authoritarian. The deadliest kind – the charming kind. The kind you want to please even when you know they're wrong. And then later, much later, you realize you've violated part of yourself. So here I am, years after his death, resisting my father's authority.

(to portrait) No, Father, it's alright to be alone with Vincent. I won't go home yet!

(to **VINCENT**) Delayed reaction, huh? But better late than never.

VINCENT. Your family always seemed so happy together. For years, I suppose, I've held you as an ideal to strive for with my own family.

MARCIA. Not an ideal – an illusion. The surface of things. Of course we *seemed* happy. After Mother died, we were rewarded with Father's approval by doing exactly what he expected of us. Father had wanted his first child to be a boy, so Olga gave up her femininity for him. With Mother gone, I became the woman of the house at fourteen – hostessing dinners and faculty gatherings – a gracious Southern belle.

VINCENT. I remember. It was charming.

MARCIA. It was unsavory. I was a midget Scarlett O'Hara, a child-prodigy Martha Stewart. It took me years to understand that it wasn't me, but a role I had adopted.

VINCENT. I'm so sorry. But you seem to have realized yourself.

MARCIA. Yes. As evidenced by my performance this evening, I've learned to become almost completely charmless, graceless, and tactless.

VINCENT. Honest, I would call it.

(**MARCIA** *looks at* **VINCENT** *for a moment – apprecia-tively.*)

MARCIA. Thank you.... I suppose I fared better than poor Andrew, who had to hand his balls over to Father. Only one pair allowed in the house, you know. After Father died, Andrew got them back; but, strangely, he keeps looking for someone else to give them to. Olga and I passed them back and forth for a while, but we really didn't want them. Finally, Andrew found a real taker in Nancy, who, it seems, had been looking for an extra pair for some time.

VINCENT. *(smiling)* And Irene?

MARCIA. Irene was so young when Father died, I really think she's emerged unscathed. Most of her recol-lections of Father are actually stories Olga and I have repeated to her – Father's Greatest Hits – or things we simply invented. Like the story she told tonight over her birthday cake. Father never said those things to her. We did.

(**VINCENT** *says nothing.*)

What? I know when someone's looking or thinking askance at me.

VINCENT. It's just that you pride yourself on your honesty, and you're brutally honest with yourself –

MARCIA. And lots of other poor unfortunate souls.

VINCENT. *(smiling)* Yes. And yet you spin fantasies for Irene.

MARCIA. Not fantasies. Simply a refined reality. Why not give her something solid to build on?

VINCENT. Because it's imaginary, fragmentary, it's not whole –and on some level, she must realize that. Ultimately, it's not a true foundation.

(**MARCIA** *is silent.*)

VINCENT. *(cont'd)* I'm sorry. Perhaps I've overstepped –

MARCIA. No, you may be right in theory. But all you have to do is look at Irene to see she turned out pretty well.

VINCENT. She's a lovely young woman.

MARCIA. She seemed to have a good time tonight, didn't she?

VINCENT. Yes, I think so.

MARCIA. Do you think my argument with Harry upset her?

VINCENT. *(smiling)* Actually, she seemed rather used to it.

MARCIA. I suppose she is. I suppose everyone is. I guess I'm really asking if it upset you.

VINCENT. Well, it's always disturbing to witness an argument – particularly if it involves someone you...admire.

(**MARCIA** *and* **VINCENT** *share a frank look.*)

MARCIA. And you can...admire someone who brawls with her husband in public?

VINCENT. Are you begging the compliment?

MARCIA. Yes. Please elaborate.

VINCENT. Alright. Your feelings toward your husband don't concern me. I find you to be a very attractive woman with strong character.

MARCIA. Is that a line that works often in your travels?

VINCENT. *(stung)* I don't have much occasion to use it.

MARCIA. I'm sorry.

VINCENT. I thought you wanted me to be frank.

MARCIA. I did. I suppose I'm just not very comfortable with your feelings – or mine. I haven't flirted with a man in years. My responses are those of a coquette from another era.

VINCENT. I have seen women outside my marriage. But my marriage isn't a happy one.

MARCIA. Whose is, when you want to get laid?

(**VINCENT** *takes this like a slap;* **MARCIA** *immediately regrets it.*)

MARCIA. *(cont'd)* I'm sorry. I've done it again. It's just a defense mechanism.

VINCENT. No. You're right. I know it sounds like a cliché used by any man on the make, but it happens to be true. I'm a lonely man in a bad marriage.

MARCIA. Please. I said I'm sorry.

VINCENT. *(continuing)* And I assure you, picking up women for sexual purposes is never this soul-wrenching or time-consuming.

MARCIA. I don't know whether to apologize, thank you, or be insulted.

VINCENT. I'm saying this is something more than a sexual thing. Do you realize that?

(**MARCIA** *nods.*)

And is the feeling mutual?

(**MARCIA** *nods again.*)

So what would you like to do?

MARCIA. Go home. *(off* **VINCENT**'s *look)* I'm really just a good girl who's more comfortable fighting with her husband than cheating on him. I guess I'd rather be a bitch than a slut.

VINCENT. Does caring about someone make you a slut?

MARCIA. Expressing it does.

(**MARCIA** *shuts one of the two remaining lights and picks up a shopping bag.*)

MARCIA. We can share a cab. Would you mind dropping me at my place?

VINCENT. I insist on it. Here, let me take that for you.

(**VINCENT** *places his hand over* **MARCIA**'s *on the handle of the shopping bag. She turns to him.*)

VINCENT. Don't be afraid of me.

MARCIA. *(in a tiny voice)* I'm not – but I am afraid.

(**VINCENT** *lowers the bag to the ground and takes* **MARCIA** *in his arms. She presses her head to his chest like a child in need of affection. After a moment, he lowers his head to hers and they kiss.*)

(**NANCY** *enters the courtyard right, walks up the steps to the terrace, and peers through the glass door to observe* **MARCIA** *and* **VINCENT** *kissing within. She smiles with satisfaction, then suddenly flings open the door.*)

(**MARCIA** *and* **VINCENT** *pull apart in shock and turn to* **NANCY** *standing in the doorway.*)

NANCY. My God, we've been calling everywhere for you!

MARCIA. Why? What's wrong? Where's Andrew?

NANCY. He's at the hospital.

MARCIA. What happened?! Is he hurt?!

NANCY. It's Irene.

MARCIA. What?!

NANCY. A drug overdose!

MARCIA. *(rushing to the door)* Oh no! Oh my God!

(Piano music, Brahms's "Hungarian Dance No. 1," rises as **VINCENT** *follows* **MARCIA** *up the stairs and out the upstage right terrace door.* **NANCY** *sweetly ponders her new advantage for a brief moment, then follows. Music swells, and curtain falls.)*

Scene 3

(Music continues as curtain rises, revealing a hospital waiting room and piece of corridor on the right side of the stage. The stage is split left and right by a wall with a closed door which adjoins a patient room left.)

(OLGA paces nervously in the waiting area. ANDREW sits in stony silence on a chair in the corner. DAVID sits beside him, legs and arms crossed, fists clenched; he glances frequently at the door leading to the patient room.)

(In the patient room, IRENE lies propped up in bed as a NURSE tends to her. An I.V. unit is connected to her wrist. IRENE is wide awake, seemingly calm, staring into space.)

(Conversation in one room cannot be heard by the characters in the other room when the door is closed, but will syncopate and occasionally overlap for the audience throughout the scene.)

(Music fades as:)

OLGA. Where the hell is everybody?!

ANDREW. Don't worry. If Nancy doesn't find Marcia at school, Marcia or Harry will get my voice-mail message.

OLGA. But she could have died, for God's sake, and nobody would have been here! She could have died all alone with strangers around her!

(ANDREW rises, crosses to OLGA and puts his arms around her.)

ANDREW. Shh. It's alright now. We're here with her. The worst is over.

(MARCIA bursts into the waiting area from the corridor right; VINCENT and NANCY trail behind her.)

MARCIA. What happened?! Is she alright?!

ANDREW. She's fine now. She's resting.

MARCIA. Where is she?

OLGA. *(angrily)* Where were *you?!*

MARCIA. I was still at the college. I told you I was going to clean up.

OLGA. For two hours?!

ANDREW. What difference does it make? We're all here now.

(to **MARCIA**, *with a gesture toward the door)*

The nurse is giving her some medication.

MARCIA. Have you seen her? Why can't I see her?

ANDREW. In just a few minutes. Let her get settled. We saw her in emergency before they brought her up.

MARCIA. Was she alright? Was she in pain?

OLGA. She could have died!

MARCIA. Would you stop punishing me and tell me what happened?!

ANDREW. She was having respiratory failure. The doctor said if they'd found her a few minutes later she would have gone into cardiac arrest.

MARCIA. Oh my God! Who found her?

DAVID. I did. I was worried about her getting home alright after the party, so I followed her to her apartment and waited across the street until she entered the lobby. I was just about to walk away, when I saw her faint.

ANDREW. She collapsed by the elevator. If David hadn't...

MARCIA. What caused it? What was it?

ANDREW. She told the doctor it was crystal meth. Speed.

OLGA. Maybe she was experimenting. Maybe she used it to study for exams.

ANDREW. She's been mainlining it – for some time now She has needle marks on both arms.

MARCIA. *(quickly)* Oh, no. I would have known.

ANDREW. We saw them, Marcia.

> (**MARCIA** *stands mute, defeated.*)

VINCENT. She'll be alright now. The important thing is that
    she got here in time.

OLGA. Thank you, Vincent. Thank you for being here.

> (*He nods.* **NANCY** *rolls her eyes.*)

OLGA. And thank you, David. Thank you so much.

MARCIA. *(numbly)* Yes, thank you, David.

DAVID. Please. I'm just so grateful I was there.

> (*Inside the patient room, the* **NURSE** *steps to* **IRENE**'s
> *bedside.*)

NURSE. *(to* **IRENE***)* Can I get you anything else?

IRENE. No. Thank you. Thank you very much.

NURSE. Do you want to go right to sleep now, or would you
    like to see your family first?

IRENE. They must be very worried. I'd like to see them first.

MARCIA. Why can't we go in?

NURSE. *(to* **IRENE***)* Alright. But just for a few minutes. You
    need a good rest.

IRENE. Thank you.

> (*The* **NURSE** *crosses to the door, exits into the waiting
> area, closes the door behind her.*)

MARCIA. *(quickly)* Is she alright?

NURSE. Yes. She'd like to see you. But no more than two at
    a time, please – for just a few minutes.

> (**MARCIA** *walks toward the door.*)

ANDREW. Olga, you go with her.

> (*The two sisters enter the room and close the door behind
> them.* **MARCIA** *rushes to the bedside and hugs* **IRENE**.
> **OLGA** *follows and brushes back Irene's hair.*)

MARCIA. Oh, my poor darling. Are you alright?

IRENE. Yes.... I'm sorry.

MARCIA. Shhh. Just relax now. You look a little pale, but
    after a good night's sleep you'll be fine.

OLGA. "Sleep that knits up the raveled sleeve of care."

(As **IRENE** *casts a questioning glance at* **OLGA**:*)*

ANDREW. *(to* **NURSE***)* Can't she come home with us tonight?

NURSE. The doctor would like her to stay overnight. If she's stable in the morning, she can leave then.

ANDREW. Thank you.

*(***NURSE** *crosses into the corridor and exits right.)*

OLGA. *(opening her purse)* Here. I got you a toothbrush downstairs.

(She places the toothbrush in **IRENE**'s *hand.)*

IRENE. Thank you.... Why haven't you asked me what happened?

OLGA. David told us.

IRENE. David? What does David know?

OLGA. He followed you home to make sure you were alright. When you collapsed in the lobby, he and the building manager got you here.

IRENE. David was following me? That's weird.

MARCIA. He helped you, darling. You should be grateful.

IRENE. Yes. I'm grateful. And surprised.

OLGA. You know David takes a brotherly interest in you. He considers himself one of the family.

IRENE. I have a family. And I don't need a chaperone.

MARCIA. Apparently you do!

IRENE. No, I don't! What I do alone is my business.

MARCIA. That's a stupid, childish thing to say!

IRENE. Appropriate behavior for someone who's treated like a child! I'm lying in the hospital after a drug overdose and you hand me a toothbrush, and when I ask you if you want to know what happened you tell me David told you. Well, what do you think David knows about my life?! Why don't you ask *me*?!

OLGA. We didn't want to upset you.

IRENE. You never want to upset me.

MARCIA. Are we supposed to read your mind? You know you can talk to us about anything.

IRENE. As long as it feeds the perception of me that you're comfortable with.

MARCIA. Is this somehow our fault?! Is that it?!

IRENE. No. It's my fault that I'm on drugs -

OLGA. You're not!

IRENE. It's your fault you can't accept it!

MARCIA. Shh. You're just tired now, darling.

IRENE. See? You'll be telling people I just had a little fainting spell, like some overwrought Southern lady.

(**SOKOL** *and* **DR. CHEBRIN** *enter the waiting area.* **DR. CHEBRIN** *seems disoriented from his sudden awakening; he wears trousers and his pajama top with a jacket thrown over them.* **SOKOL** *is disheveled and wild-eyed with concern.*)

SOKOL. Where is she?

ANDREW. She's alright.

(*gesturing*)

She's in there with Olga and Marcia. She just needs some rest. Doctor, I didn't mean for you to come to the hospital. I was simply trying to find Marcia.

DR. CHEBRIN. How could I not come?

SOKOL. What happened?

ANDREW. She...she overdosed on crystal meth. Apparently it was accidental.

SOKOL. Yeah. Tell that one to Dr. Freud.

DAVID. You can't control your sarcasm under any circumstances, can you?

SOKOL. Look, I hate to shatter your Norman Rockwell view of the world, but people who drug themselves to overdose are trying to kill themselves.

DAVID. (*rising, angry*) Who are you to assign motives to her? What do you know about her?

SOKOL. More than you could handle.

DR. CHEBRIN. Both of you stop this right now.

DAVID. *(to* **SOKOL***)* Everything looks warped from where you stand – but the distortion is internal, not external.

DR. CHEBRIN. What's the matter with you two? You're friends, for God's sake.

ANDREW. Yes, please stop arguing.

VINCENT. You're both tired and upset.

SOKOL. *(with his eyes on* **DAVID***)* Is that what it is?

DR. CHEBRIN. *(to* **ANDREW***)* How did she get here?

ANDREW. David found her in her apartment lobby and called the paramedics.

SOKOL. *(suspicious)* What was David doing in her apartment lobby?

DAVID. I walked her home.

SOKOL. She left the party by herself.

DAVID. I followed her to make sure she'd be alright.

SOKOL. Do you have a sixth sense about potential drug overdoses?

ANDREW. What are you bickering about? Thank God David was there.

DAVID. *(to* **SOKOL***)* Looking after someone must be an incomprehensible concept to you.

SOKOL. Don't dignify your perversions to me, you creep.

*(***DAVID*** flies at* **SOKOL***. The two scuffle for a moment before* **VINCENT***,* **DR. CHEBRIN***, and* **ANDREW*** pull them apart.)*

NANCY. Jesus, stop it!

ANDREW. Enough!

(to **SOKOL***)*

I'll have to ask you to leave, Gary.

SOKOL. *(straightening his shirt and brushing his hair back)* Really, Andrew? Are you the hospital bouncer?

*(***MARCIA*** and* **OLGA*** enter the waiting area from* **IRENE***'s room and close the door behind them.)*

MARCIA. What's going on out here?

ANDREW. Nothing. Dr. Chebrin and Gary arrived, and everyone's very concerned about Irene.

DR. CHEBRIN. *(to* **MARCIA***)* How is she?

MARCIA. She's going to be alright, Doctor.

OLGA. I think it was the pressure of finals. She needed a release from the pressure.

SOKOL. Are you the spin doctor? She taking image consulting from you, Mr. Antonelli?

DAVID. Shut the fuck up!

(then, quickly)

Excuse me, ladies.

ANDREW. I don't think we have to distort things for our friends, Olga.

NANCY. Yes, we're all family here. Even Mr. Antonelli knew you from childhood,

(with a look to **MARCIA***)*

and he's gotten much closer this evening.

*(***HARRY** *strides into the waiting area from the corridor.)*

HARRY. What's going on? Is she alright?

MARCIA. She's resting.

HARRY. Well, what happened, for God's sake?

ANDREW. She overdosed on crystal meth. David found her.

SOKOL. After lurking about for a few hours –

DAVID. Would you *SHUT UP?!*

SOKOL. *(continuing)* Waiting for an opportunity to assert his fragile masculinity.

*(***DAVID** *throws a magazine at* **SOKOL***.* **SOKOL** *starts for* **DAVID***.* **VINCENT** *stops him.)*

HARRY. Have you both gone crazy?

MARCIA. He says that to everyone, hoping to increase his business.

VINCENT. Everyone's nerves are a little frayed, that's all.

ANDREW. *(pointing to* **SOKOL***)* This one's out of his fucking mind tonight!

HARRY. *(to* **ANDREW***)* She overdosed. David found her. That's it?

MARCIA. You get here this late, you get a short synopsis.

HARRY. The heart of concern. I'm asking about your goddamn *sister!*

ANDREW. Don't start this here, both of you.

MARCIA. *(ignoring* **ANDREW***, to* **HARRY***)* You left my goddamn sister's birthday party to be with the goddamn *Waldmanns,* so don't stroll in at the eleventh hour with your professional arrogance and your righteous indignation expecting all the lay persons to give you oral reports. You're not the doctor here, Harry – just another guy who missed the show.

NANCY. *(to* **HARRY***)* Actually, Marcia was a little late, too – if that makes you feel any better.

MARCIA. *(to* **NANCY***)* Not as good as it makes *you* feel.

ANDREW. I'm going to see my sister.

(*to* **OLGA**)

Is she still awake?

OLGA. Yes.

DR. CHEBRIN. Everybody on the floor's awake now.

ANDREW. Would you like to come in with me, Doctor?

SOKOL. He's half dressed, half asleep, and half drunk. That's all she needs.

OLGA. Really, Gary. Is no one free from these little cacas you seem compelled to make in public?

SOKOL. Just give her a little privacy, that's all.

(**ANDREW** *starts for the door, turns to* **NANCY** *and* **DR. CHEBRIN**.)

ANDREW. Nancy? Doctor?

(**NANCY** *nods and follows* **ANDREW**.)

DR. CHEBRIN. I...I'll wait out here. Just give her my love.

DAVID. *(to* **SOKOL***)* Way to go.

(As **ANDREW** *and* **NANCY** *enter* **IRENE***'s room,* **OLGA** *sees* **HARRY** *eyeing* **VINCENT** *and:)*

OLGA. Harry, please meet an old family friend...

(As the two men approach each other and shake hands:)

*(***ANDREW** *and* **NANCY** *walk to Irene's bedside. She smiles weakly at them.* **ANDREW** *takes her hand and strokes it.)*

ANDREW. Feeling a little better?

*(***IRENE** *nods.)*

NANCY. Gosh, we were so worried about you, but you look great – really great. Just a little pale. But you'll be out tomorrow and you'll feel, you know – *great.*

IRENE. Thanks, Nancy.

ANDREW. Can we get you anything?

IRENE. No. Thank you.

DR. CHEBRIN. I guess I'll go home. What good is an old man in a crisis?

*(***DAVID** *shoots a hateful glance at* **SOKOL.***)*

MARCIA. Thank you for coming, Doctor. It will mean a lot to Irene to know you were here.

DR. CHEBRIN. Hah! Who knows anything. This whole thing may have been a dream. We may all wake up tomorrow having had the same bad dream.

SOKOL. I don't think metaphysics are going to save us from this one.

*(***DR. CHEBRIN** *kisses* **OLGA** *and* **MARCIA** *good night.)*

DAVID. Can I walk you downstairs, Doctor?

SOKOL. He's good at that.

DR. CHEBRIN. Thank you, but I get in an elevator, I get in a cab. I can handle that. Good night.

(He begins to exit, then stops in front of **SOKOL.***)*

DR. CHEBRIN. I think your mother must have dropped you when you were a baby, and something broke *(taps* **SOKOL***'s chest over his heart)* in here.

SOKOL. Although never literally, I've been dropped a few
    times, Doctor.

DR. CHEBRIN. *(nodding)* It shows.

   *(**DR. CHEBRIN** exits.)*

HARRY. *(to **MARCIA**)* How much longer are you going to
    stay?

MARCIA. I don't know. You don't have to. In fact, please
    don't.

HARRY. I don't want you leaving here alone at a late hour.

MARCIA. Please. All this obligatory gallantry is tiresome.
    You know I can take care of myself.

HARRY. What I know is that your defensive skills are mostly
    verbal.

OLGA. Andrew and I will drop her off.

VINCENT. Or I'd be happy to see her home.

   *(**HARRY** looks from **MARCIA** to **VINCENT** for a moment.)*

HARRY. I see....

   *(to **MARCIA**)*

   What better protection than nostalgia personified.
   Good night.

   *(**HARRY** exits.)*

IRENE. Andrew, you know what I'd like?

ANDREW. What, darling? Tell me, I'll call the nurse.

IRENE. No. She can't give it to me.... I want to go back to
    Charleston for a little while. All of us. Spend some
    time in the house. Find our old souls. Inhabit our old
    space. Do you think we could do that?

ANDREW. I...sure...I think we could. The current lease will
    be up in a few months, and as soon as the tenants are
    out we could fly down.

   *(**NANCY** shoots **ANDREW** a cautionary look.)*

IRENE. *(growing more excited)* Or maybe we could drive down
    and see the countryside. I'd like that. See the leaves
    changing, stop at antique shops and farmers' markets
    on the way.

ANDREW. That sounds lovely, darling. Shhh. You relax now. We'll make all the arrangements when you're better. We'll say good night now.

IRENE. Alright.

ANDREW. Would you like David to come in before you go to sleep? Just for a moment, so you can thank him?

IRENE. *(uneasy at the suggestion)* Oh...

ANDREW. You don't have to.

IRENE. No, I should. Please ask him to come in.

ANDREW. Alright.

(kisses her)

Good night, darling. You'll be my shiny new penny again in the morning.

IRENE. Thank you. Thank you both.

(NANCY gives IRENE a kiss on the cheek.)

NANCY. Get a good night's sleep and everything will be –

IRENE. I know – great.

NANCY. Yeah.

VINCENT. *(to MARCIA)* I, uh...I should call my wife and kids.

MARCIA. Vincent, I'm sorry, how insensitive of me. Please, you don't have to wait here with me.

VINCENT. No, I'd like to. I'll just go down to the lobby and call. I'll wait there for you.

MARCIA. Really, you don't have to.

VINCENT. *(smiling)* I know – you're self-sufficient. I'll be downstairs.

(He exits. ANDREW and NANCY enter the waiting area from IRENE's room. All eyes turn to them.)

ANDREW. Irene would like to see you..., David.

(DAVID sits surprised, delighted for a moment, then rises and walks swiftly into the room and closes the door behind him.)

(**SOKOL** *seems stunned. He rises, looks at everyone in the room as if about to speak, then suddenly turns and exits through the corridor right.*)

NANCY. That guy gives me the creeps.

MARCIA. He just has trouble expressing himself.

ANDREW. He expresses himself too well, if you ask me.

(**DAVID** *walks hesitantly to* **IRENE**'s *bedside.*)

IRENE. It's okay, David. You can come in.

DAVID. How are you?

OLGA. *(to* **ANDREW***)* How is she?

ANDREW. Fine. She'll be fine. She wants to go to Charleston.

IRENE. *(to* **DAVID***)* I'm alright now.

OLGA. Why?

ANDREW. She wants to become a child again. Escape her current problem. That's pretty obvious, isn't it.

MARCIA. God, Andrew, you sound just like Harry – cold and academic.

ANDREW. Maybe that's the antidote for the world of emotion you force everyone to inhabit. A little dignity and self control wouldn't hurt –

MARCIA. Stop. You made your point.

ANDREW. I'm wiped out. Are you coming with us?

MARCIA. I'll stay here for a while.

ANDREW. We should let her get to sleep.

MARCIA. Just a while.

NANCY. Where's Vincent?

MARCIA. I'm too tired for your bullshit now, Nancy. Just go home.

ANDREW. It's strange. I don't even expect you to be civil anymore. How sad for you.

MARCIA. Oh, don't cry for me.

ANDREW. Olga, are you coming?

OLGA. I'll stay with Marcia.

ANDREW. Then, good night.

(He kisses both sisters on the cheek. **MARCIA** *takes his hand to stop him as he turns away. She speaks in an uncharacteristically meek and quiet voice.)*

MARCIA. I'm sorry.

*(***ANDREW*** shakes his head, troubled, and exits with* **NANCY** *in tow.)*

OLGA. Why do you do it, Marcia? You terrorize everyone and then you apologize.

MARCIA. I don't terrorize everyone, and I don't apologize to everyone I terrorize. You could have left with him, you know.

OLGA. I want to be with my sister.

MARCIA. Which one?

OLGA. I don't know which of you worries me more.

IRENE. *(to* **DAVID***)* Thank you for helping me.

DAVID. Please, you don't have to thank me.

IRENE. Apparently, if it weren't for you –

DAVID. Please, stop. Don't even talk about it.

(She takes his hand.)

IRENE. Please. Let me thank you. You helped me. You might have saved my life. Thank you.

DAVID. You're...you're welcome.

OLGA. Why would she do something like that? And how could we not know about it.

MARCIA. We all carry our secrets, I guess. Don't we have secrets from her?

OLGA. You? You don't have any secrets. You tell everybody everything.

MARCIA. Do I?

OLGA. If there's more, I'm not sure I want to hear about it.

MARCIA. I know. You never did.

OLGA. What does that mean?

MARCIA. Nothing. I don't want to make you uncomfortable. I know how you hate that.

OLGA. No, please continue. Don't spare me. Tell me I'm responsible for your psychological turmoil and your bad marriage.

(The sisters stop and stare at one another.)

MARCIA. Is that what *you* think? Crie de coeur.

OLGA. I don't need this. Go home and do this with your husband.

MARCIA. You'd like that, wouldn't you. You probably hoped, when I married him, that he'd solve all our problems.

OLGA. *Our* problems?

MARCIA. What Father did to me is your problem, too, Olga. And now, in some strange way, I think it's even become Irene's.

OLGA. If spewing vitriol for eternity is your way of coming to terms with what happened to you, then it's become *everyone's* problem.

MARCIA. It's not "what *happened* to me," Olga. It's what Father *did* to me.

OLGA. Alright! I accepted that a year ago. I believed you even though Father wasn't there to defend himself.

DAVID. *(to* **IRENE***)* Can I get you anything?

IRENE. No, I'm...quite comfortable, thank you.

MARCIA. You insult me in so many subtle ways. As if I were Father's posthumous persecutor.

OLGA. What's the point in going over and over it?!

MARCIA. It's not finished! It's never finished until you accept it!

OLGA. I told you I did! But I loved him. He was my father. And he didn't do those things to me.

(Pause.)

MARCIA. Exactly. He didn't do those things to you.

OLGA. What does *that* mean?

MARCIA. It means you knew what he was doing to me long before I told you. You knew as a child. While it was happening.

OLGA. That's a lie!

MARCIA. And on some level, you were jealous.

OLGA. This is so twisted.

MARCIA. And you've lived with that jealousy and your feelings of inadequacy for years. They've created a barrier between you and me, you and Irene, and you and yourself.

(**OLGA** *rises.*)

OLGA. If Vincent is seeing you home, I might as well leave.

(**OLGA** *starts to exit.* **MARCIA** *rises and takes her hand to restrain her.*)

MARCIA. Please listen for Irene if not for me. We really haven't given her the foundation she spoke of tonight. It's a quicksand of myths and half-truths. You and I have learned to live with it with just enough success to get by – a bitter, frustrated woman exorcising her demons with verbal assaults and a closet lesbian trying to be the father she loved and hated.

(**OLGA** *wrenches her hand from* **MARCIA**'s *grasp.*)

OLGA. My sexual orientation is my business. And it's a necessary secret for a school teacher.

MARCIA. If you want to think so. But why have you never discussed it with Irene? And only by inference with me?

OLGA. Why should I? Why expose myself to your pop psychology? Poor Olga, trying to be Father because he didn't love her enough to molest her. Bullshit!

MARCIA. Is it?

OLGA. Yes. You don't understand my complexities enough to analyze and categorize me.

MARCIA. Alright. Share them with me. Let me see you.

OLGA. I'm not sure I trust you enough.

(*The two sisters stare at each other for a moment.*)

DAVID. You look so tired. I'll let you get some sleep now.

IRENE. Thank you. Good night.

DAVID. Good night.

(he turns to go, then stops and turns back)

Do you, uh...

IRENE. Yes?

DAVID. Would you, uh, like to have dinner sometime or go to a movie?

IRENE. Uh...sure.

DAVID. You don't have to – I mean, just to be nice.

IRENE. I'd like to, David.

DAVID. *(smiling)* Okay. I'll call you. Good night.

IRENE. Good night.

(DAVID exits, elated, and closes the door behind him as he enters the waiting area.)

(MARCIA and OLGA turn to him.)

MARCIA. How is she now?

DAVID. Fine. She's going to sleep.

OLGA. *(to MARCIA)* Should we look in on her?

MARCIA. No, let's let her rest. We'll see her in the morning.

(OLGA nods, then reaches for MARCIA and kisses her on the cheek.)

(MARCIA appears confused) Don't say good night. I'm going with you.

OLGA. I wasn't saying good night.

(MARCIA suddenly understands OLGA's gesture of affection. She touches her cheek where OLGA kissed her.)

MARCIA. Oh...

(then)

Come, David. Let's go home.

(The three of them exit. The stage is quiet for a moment. IRENE has fallen asleep.)

(The **NURSE** *enters, quietly opens the door to* **IRENE**'s *room, checks her IV, dims the bedside lamp, and exits the room, leaving the door open a crack. She then crosses through the waiting area and exits right.)*

(A moment later, **SOKOL** *steals into the waiting area. He hesitates outside Irene's door for a moment, then enters silently. He stands at the foot of the bed and watches her sleep for a few seconds, then:)*

SOKOL. *(quietly)* I love you.

(Piano music rises as curtain falls.)

ACT II

*(Piano music, Chopin's "Mazurka, Opus 63, No. 3,"
rises as curtain rises on Manhattan Crest College faculty
lounge. Four months later.)*

*(**DR. CHEBRIN** is seated in the leather armchair downstage right, reading his paper beside a glowing fire. **GARY
SOKOL** is seated at the conference table in the mezzanine.
He corrects a stack of blue books and occasionally refers
to a few political science texts on the table. A bleak fall
day is visible through the mezzanine bay window.)*

*(Music fades as **DR. CHEBRIN** speaks without looking
up from his newspaper.)*

DR. CHEBRIN. Ah! A man in Tribeca cut off his best friend's
thumb for beating him at pinball!

*(**SOKOL** casts an annoyed glance at **DR. CHEBRIN** and
returns to his work.)*

His best friend!

(pause)

His *thumb!!*

*(**SOKOL** opens his mouth as if to speak, thinks better of
it, draws a deep breath, and resumes working.)*

Ah! A woman in Riverdale was raped by a man with
whom she had refused to go to their high-school prom
–ten years ago!

*(**SOKOL** clenches his fists and bites his lip.)*

Imagine carrying around that kind of resentment for
ten years.

*(**SOKOL** forces himself to relax and returns to his work.)*

DR. CHEBRIN. *(cont'd)* Ah! Three Carmelite nuns in Brooklyn –

SOKOL. *(exploding)* Would you *SHUT UP!*

DR. CHEBRIN. What...?

SOKOL. I don't give a contortionist's fuck what happened to three Carmelite nuns in Brooklyn!

DR. CHEBRIN. Why, I wasn't even talking to you.

SOKOL. I'm the only person unfortunate enough to be sharing this room with you right now.

DR. CHEBRIN. I was reading to myself.

SOKOL. At fifty decibels! You know, this isn't called the Reading-Out-Loud Room, or the Atrocity Room. It's called the Faculty Lounge. Why don't you just *lounge?!*

DR. CHEBRIN. Why don't you correct your papers in your office?

SOKOL. Because I'm not disturbing anyone! If you haven't mastered silent reading skills, *you* go to *your* office!

(**DR. CHEBRIN** *glares indignantly at* **SOKOL** *for a moment.* **SOKOL** *returns to his blue books.*)

DR. CHEBRIN. Ah! That's alright. I understand.

(**SOKOL** *turns slowly toward* **DR. CHEBRIN**.)

SOKOL. What exactly do you understand, old man?

DR. CHEBRIN. Your short temper, your poor manners – shorter and poorer, I should say. I understand where they're coming from.

SOKOL. Really? Enlighten me.

DR. CHEBRIN. Perhaps a certain jealousy over a certain young lady's interest in a certain *other* young man – or *his* in *her.*

(*With one swift movement,* **SOKOL** *lifts a large text from the table and hurls it across the room at* **DR. CHEBRIN**, *missing his head by inches.*)

SOKOL. Shut the fuck up, you stupid old fool!!

(OLGA and IRENE, carrying shopping bags and a cake box, enter the courtyard and cross up the terrace steps as:)

DR. CHEBRIN. *(standing, stunned)* You crazy little bastard! You could have killed me!

(The upstage right door opens, and OLGA enters with IRENE. IRENE seems more mature, but lacks some of the spirit she displayed in the opening scene.)

(As IRENE closes the door, the sisters stop, aware of the face-off between SOKOL and DR. CHEBRIN.)

OLGA. What happened? What's going on?

SOKOL. Nothing. I just dropped my book.

DR. CHEBRIN. One of those fifteen-foot gravity-defying drops!

(As SOKOL crosses downstairs to pick up the text – and to avoid the questioning stares of the sisters:)

SOKOL. I'll call Ripley's as soon as I get to my office.

(SOKOL bends down and scoops up the book at DR. CHEBRIN's feet. CHEBRIN speaks to him quietly but angrily.)

DR. CHEBRIN. You could have killed me.

SOKOL. And let you become one of your precious headlines? "Ah! English professor killed by flying political science text!" I wouldn't give you the postmortem satisfaction.

(SOKOL dashes back up the stairs and quickly gathers his books and papers.)

I have some papers to grade.

IRENE. Don't let us force you out.

SOKOL. I work better in my office.

IRENE. Why don't you stay and join us? We're having a little party.

SOKOL. Another soul-stripping tribal dance by the Prior family? What's the special occasion?

OLGA. A baby shower for Andrew and Nancy.

SOKOL. Oh God. Have they performed an amniocentesis to find out what species it's going to be?

*(**IRENE** stifles a chuckle. **OLGA** gives her a stern look, then to **SOKOL**:)*

OLGA. Mr. Sokol, I don't appreciate your responding to an invitation by insulting all of the members of my family, including the unborn.

SOKOL. Do you think being chancellor entitles you to give me deportment lessons?

OLGA. Yes! And I won't have you throwing books at other teachers.

SOKOL. The Fuhrer meets Emily Post. Maybe I'll stop by later for some practical lessons in behavior from the rest of the family.

*(**SOKOL** exits, leaving one text on the table. **OLGA** angrily removes party items from a bag. **IRENE** assists her.)*

OLGA. That insufferable little man! He almost begs me to fire him.

IRENE. He doesn't care. Can't you see that?

OLGA. Why not? What tragedy in his life has destroyed his mechanism for self-preservation?

IRENE. He simply doesn't care about things that most people care about.

DR. CHEBRIN. Or he cares too much.

OLGA. Did he hurt you, Doctor?

DR. CHEBRIN. No, no. It's not me he's angry at. I'm just a convenient target.

OLGA. Who is it, then? Humanity in general?

DR. CHEBRIN. It's more specific than that.

IRENE. It's me, isn't it?

OLGA. You? Why would he be angry at you?

IRENE. It *is* me, isn't it, Doctor?

DR. CHEBRIN. My dear, you could only be an object of love to any man. Not anger.

OLGA. I don't believe it. He isn't capable of love.

DR. CHEBRIN. Every man has silent dreams he doesn't share with the world, delicate longings he fears will be shattered by derision. Why should Gary be immune to such feelings? Because he shouts and makes snide remarks? Those aren't his emotions; they are his hiding place.

IRENE. So the object of love becomes the object of scorn.

DR. CHEBRIN. No. The object of *your* love becomes the object of his scorn.

IRENE. David?

(**DR. CHEBRIN** *nods.*)

OLGA. How do you know this, Doctor?

DR. CHEBRIN. I know nothing more than you do, my dear. I simply acknowledge the truth when it presents itself to me. Excuse me, I have some paperwork to attend to.

(**DR. CHEBRIN** *turns and ascends the left staircase.*)

OLGA. Won't you stay for the party, Doctor? Nothing elaborate, just a toast to Andrew and Nancy.

DR. CHEBRIN. Perhaps I've never told you, but I despise that young woman.

OLGA. Oh, so do we all. But please come for our sake. We need good spirits when she's around. Like at an exorcism.

DR. CHEBRIN. I'll stop by to toast evolution. In Nancy's case, it's a dire necessity.

(**DR. CHEBRIN** *exits through upstage left door.*)

(**IRENE** *walks downstairs.* **OLGA** *follows.*)

IRENE. David and Gary were good friends.

OLGA. Please don't blame yourself.

IRENE. I'd hate to be responsible for any hostility between them.

OLGA. Hostility? What could happen between two edu-
cated, civilized men? A chess match to the death?
Don't be morbid.

IRENE. It isn't as if David and I were the romance of the
century. What's there to be so jealous of?

OLGA. You're engaged to the man, dear, aren't you?

IRENE. Yes....

OLGA. So Gary's out of luck. It's as simple as that. Unless
you're not really committed to this engagement.

IRENE. Of course I am. I am. But the intensity of my
feelings for David –

OLGA. *(interrupting)* Nobody knows the intensity of your
feelings and nobody should. It's not published with
the marriage banns. So don't expect Gary to be less
jealous because you don't love David as much as you
think you should.

IRENE. As much as he loves me.

OLGA. Somehow, over time, it equalizes itself. Love is never
the way it's presented in fiction. We arrive at it with so
little experience and so many false expectations. Don't
agonize over it. Trust your decision.

(As IRENE *and* OLGA *continue to speak,* MARCIA *and*
VINCENT *appear in the courtyard and pause at the foot
of the terrace steps.* MARCIA *gazes up at the sky. Dialogue
between interior and exterior is not audible to the characters in the other area.)*

MARCIA. These fall days are so precious. We never know
how many we have left before winter.

(As MARCIA *and* VINCENT *begin to walk up the terrace
steps:)*

IRENE. It's not me I'm worried about. I have no illusions
anymore. I don't expect a white knight. It's David. He
deserves better.

OLGA. David's doing quite well for himself, thank you very
much. He's won a prize with you – he's grabbed the
ring on the carousel.

IRENE. Brass. No timbre, no sparkle. I'm settling for security, and he knows it.

OLGA. How does he know it?

IRENE. I told him.

(OLGA is disturbed by this. She moves to **IRENE** *and takes her hands.)*

OLGA. Darling, discretion is called for, even in intimate relationships. Don't make honesty an excuse for unburdening yourself of unwanted thoughts and emotions. That's what your sister does, and her marriage has become a sideshow.

(As they reach the terrace level, **MARCIA** *turns to* **VINCENT**, *sees the troubled expression on his face.)*

MARCIA. What is it? What's wrong?

VINCENT. I had a conversation with Helen today – an unpleasant one.

MARCIA. About us?

(VINCENT nods.)

What about us, Vincent?

(As **VINCENT** *heaves a sigh and begins to speak (inaudible to the audience)* **MARCIA**'s *expression grows from wary curiosity to dismay. They are not yet visible to* **OLGA** *and* **IRENE**, *who continue their conversation in the main room:)*

IRENE. I couldn't start our life together with a lie.

OLGA. But what's the truth, anyway? Sometimes it's just a verbalization of our surface fears and insecurities. But once spoken, the words define our reality.

IRENE. *(pulling away from her sister)* That's the reality I have to inhabit now. I'm in recovery, Olga. I'm fighting to stay out of the fantasy world of drugs and delusions I inhabited. And honest words, however imperfect, are my only tool for getting back, and for keeping my world straight.

(she pauses, then more gently)

IRENE. Can you understand that?

OLGA. *(nodding)* Yes.

IRENE. We want to move to Charleston.

OLGA. Charleston?

IRENE. Why not? We've talked about it all these years. David could get a job in the philosophy department at State. We could stay at the house...that is, if it's alright with you and Marcia and Andrew.

OLGA. Of course! Why not? The current lease is up soon. You'll move in and make a real home of it again, complete with sisters who visit and stay too long.

IRENE. Never too long.

(IRENE and OLGA embrace. As they do, MARCIA reacts in horror to something VINCENT has told her, then embraces him desperately.)

(As OLGA and IRENE separate, IRENE sees MARCIA and VINCENT through the terrace door.)

IRENE. Look.

OLGA. *(turning)* My God, right in the courtyard. How indiscreet.

IRENE. No. Something's wrong.

(MARCIA and VINCENT break their embrace. VINCENT tries to console her. MARCIA pulls away from him, and, as she turns, sees her sisters through the door. She quickly composes herself, opens the door, and enters the mezzanine. VINCENT follows as MARCIA steps to the top of the right staircase and speaks down to IRENE and OLGA:)

MARCIA. Vincent's leaving today.

IRENE. For where?

MARCIA. "Where" doesn't matter. "Why" is the question.

VINCENT. *(interrupting)* Baltimore. My work here is –

MARCIA. *(turning sharply)* What? You still here?

(then, to her sisters)

His work has very little to do with it.

IRENE. *(anxiously)* When are you coming back?

MARCIA. Never. He's never coming back. At least not to me, not to us.

VINCENT. Please, Marcia.

MARCIA. Oh, I'm sorry. Was I wrong? Correct me if I'm wrong.

VINCENT. Go ahead. If this has to end with open wounds for you, go ahead.

MARCIA. *(to* **VINCENT***)* This wasn't my idea.

(to **IRENE** *and* **OLGA***)*

Actually, it wasn't Vincent's, either. It was his poor, crazy wife's idea.

(to **VINCENT***)*

You don't mind if I call her that, do you?

*(***VINCENT** *stares quietly at* **MARCIA***. She meets his stare for a moment, then turns to her sisters and continues.)*

It seems that poor, crazy Helen was praying one day, when God told her to take her two little girls away from their slut-mongering father. So it was really God's idea, and guess what that makes *me!* Anyway, even a certifiable loony like Helen would win custody of the girls in a divorce proceeding—what with Vincent having boffed me a few times a week for several months now. Better a crazy mother than a corrupt father, I guess.

OLGA. Marcia, stop this. End it with a little dignity.

MARCIA. I'm fresh out! But I'm almost through. So, divorce was out, because Vincent loves the girls and crazy Helen knows it. And murdering crazy Helen was out, because Vincent is one of those *sensitive* husbands. So that left deserting me.

VINCENT. You know I love you, Marcia. You know this is tearing me up.

MARCIA. Oh, I know. But you can't have both. Like when I was a little girl. Father said, "You can't have the chocolate bunny *and* the glazed Easter egg." But I cried for both and I got nothing. So you see, you're right, Vincent. You're doing the *sensible* thing.

(MARCIA *turns from* VINCENT *and descends the right staircase.*)

VINCENT. *(to* IRENE *and* OLGA*)* I can't give up my girls, you know. Not simply because I don't want to be deprived of their company. It's not that selfish. I can't have them growing up under their mother's influence. They're such good, bright girls. It would be too destructive for them. So I have to make the sacrifice. And, unfortunately, so does Marcia. If there were any way I could bear this alone, believe me, I would....

(He stops, overcome, then quickly gathers himself and continues.)

I've enjoyed making your acquaintance again as adults. I hope my girls grow up to be as close and mutually supportive as you three sisters. And...I love your sister – deeply. Otherwise, it never would have come to this. I hope you believe that.

(MARCIA *seems close to tears, but she controls herself and will not look at* VINCENT.)

IRENE. Of course we do, Vincent.

OLGA. Yes, of course.

VINCENT. Thank you.... Well...

(He walks down the stairs, takes OLGA*'s hand and kisses it.)*

Goodbye, Olga. I know you'll make a fine chancellor.

OLGA. Thank you, Vincent. Goodbye.

VINCENT. *(takes* IRENE*'s hand and kisses it)* Goodbye, Irene. I hope you and David will be happy.

IRENE. Thank you, Vincent. I hope you will be, too.

VINCENT. Thank you.

(VINCENT *pauses awkwardly, turns to* MARCIA.)

Marcia, will you walk me out and help me find a cab?

(MARCIA *will not speak or turn to look at* VINCENT. *She shakes her head, "No."*)

VINCENT. *(cont'd)* I see. Well...

> *(crosses to* **MARCIA** *and utters quietly:)*

Goodbye, my girl.

> *(***VINCENT** *turns and crosses up the right staircase, pauses at the terrace door, then turns back one last time.* **MARCIA** *does not turn or move.)*

OLGA. *(quietly)* Marcia, please...

> *(***MARCIA** *again slowly shakes her head "No."* **VINCENT** *turns in despair and exits through the upstage right door, closes it, crosses the terrace, and begins descending the steps to the courtyard.)*

> *(At the sound of the door closing,* **MARCIA** *turns. She looks up at the closed door in panic and murmurs to herself:)*

MARCIA. Vincent...

> *(She rushes past her sisters, up the right staircase, opens the terrace door, and calls:)*

Vincent!

> *(***VINCENT** *stops at the base of the steps and turns as* **MARCIA** *rushes down the steps to him. He opens his arms and she flies into them, hugging him tightly, fighting unsuccessfully to hold back her tears. He tries to console her:)*

VINCENT. My girl...my sweet girl.

> *(After a few moments,* **MARCIA**, *with a great effort, stops, pulls herself up straight, and wipes her face with both hands.)*

MARCIA. There. I'm alright now.

> *(attempting a bright face)*

Come. We'll put you in a cab.

> *(As* **MARCIA** *and* **VINCENT** *exit right:)*

IRENE. My God, what's going to happen to her now?

OLGA. She'll get over it, that's all. People get over things. You did. Your sister can. She's very strong.

IRENE. Outwardly.

OLGA. She's very strong.

(MARCIA *reenters the courtyard alone, ascends the terrace steps, quietly opens the upstage rights door, and drifts back into the mezzanine. She stops, disoriented, at the balustrade, then focuses on her sisters below.*)

MARCIA. He's gone. Four months.... All love songs must be written during the first four months of a relationship.

OLGA. It had to happen eventually, Marcia. You knew that. You must have been prepared for this.

MARCIA. Yes. The same way I'm prepared for the eventuality of death. That's how prepared I am.

OLGA. "Though lovers be lost, love shall not." It'll get better. Slowly.

(MARCIA *turns a cold eye on her sister and crosses down the right staircase.*)

MARCIA. Really? What do you know about it?

OLGA. Don't turn on me because you're upset.

MARCIA. No, really. I want to know what you know about it. Console me from your vast storehouse of emotional experience.

OLGA. Just skip it. If you need to swim in your own bile to revive your spirit, go ahead. But do it by yourself.

IRENE. Marcia, Olga's trying to help you.

MARCIA. The same way she always helps. With her intellectual platitudes and her literary allusions. A little Milton or Edna St. Vincent Millay when the chips are down.

OLGA. Do you think you're the only one who's ever loved someone and said goodbye and had to get on with her life? Just because I haven't paraded all my lovers by you and argued with them and cried over them –

MARCIA. *(interrupting)* Don't parade them all. Parade just one. Argue with and cry over just *one* for me!

OLGA. No. Histrionics are *your* department!

IRENE. Stop. Both of you. What are you doing?

MARCIA. *(ignoring **IRENE**)* There's a space between histrionics and cold tit. Try inhabiting it sometime.

OLGA. I have. You just weren't present when it happened. When I fall in love, no one smiles and congratulates; they smirk and disparage. And when the affair is over, no one consoles, they sigh with relief and call it inevitable.

IRENE. I would never do that, Olga.

MARCIA. Neither would I.

OLGA. I wonder.

MARCIA. But how would you know? You never had enough trust in us to test us.

*(**OLGA** looks at her sisters for a moment, then turns away.)*

*(Pause. **OLGA** takes a breath and begins speaking to **MARCIA** without turning.)*

OLGA. I'm sorry about Vincent, Marcia. I know how much — *(She turns to face **MARCIA**.)* I'm just very sorry.

*(**MARCIA** nods.)*

MARCIA. Thank you.

*(**ANDREW** and **NANCY** enter the courtyard and stop at the base of the steps. **NANCY** is quite visibly pregnant. They speak conspiratorially:)*

NANCY. Now, don't be nervous. Just tell them it's *good news*.

*(She removes a manila envelope from her purse and hands it to **ANDREW**. He takes it, draws a deep breath, and sighs:)*

ANDREW. Okay.

*(As he turns and crosses up the steps to the terrace, **NANCY** remains at the base of the steps.)*

(She watches him intently as he bolsters himself, then enters the upstage right door.)

ANDREW. *(cont'd)* Well, I have good...

> *(He stops, aware of the mood in the room.)*

What's the matter?

MARCIA. Nothing.

> *(As he crosses down the right staircase.)*

ANDREW. You look terrible. What is it?

MARCIA. The aging process.

> *(then, flippantly, to escape his questioning)*

So, where's the barracuda?

ANDREW. Are you referring to my wife, your sister-in-law, the mother of your nephew?

MARCIA. I'm not related to fetuses, regardless of gender; but, yes, I was referring to that woman.

ANDREW. Fuck you.

OLGA. Andrew, please!

ANDREW. Well she's too much. She treats my marriage with the same irreverence she treats her own.

IRENE. Andrew, leave her alone. She's upset right now.

ANDREW. Oh, *right now?* She's *always* upset! It's her constant state. And her favorite. She wouldn't have another one if you paid her.

MARCIA. Strange, we seem to be growing more alike –

ANDREW. A disturbing thought.

MARCIA. – as we grow further apart.

ANDREW. What happened?

MARCIA. None of your goddamn business.

ANDREW. *(to OLGA and IRENE)* Will one of you tell me what happened?

IRENE. Vincent –

MARCIA. *(interrupting)* Don't.

ANDREW. Vincent what? Vincent's wife made another feeble attempt at suicide – this time by holding a paper bag over her head? Vincent's daughters placed first and second in the Glorious Youth Competition? Vincent smiled? Vincent burped?

MARCIA. I'm sorry to have overburdened you with the inconsequentials of my affair with Vincent. I did it to avoid the deeper issues I wasn't comfortable discussing with you. You've become a stranger to me – a genetic acquaintance.

OLGA. Marcia, stop.

(to **ANDREW***)*

She doesn't mean that.

ANDREW. Yes, she does. And it's true. For all of you. You've all made me a stranger. Simply because I made *one* decision without your approval!

MARCIA. Don't congratulate yourself too heartily, you stupid little boy, for marrying that low-life bitch. And don't confuse slavery with love.

ANDREW. Shut up!

MARCIA. Good answer. You think we fulfill ourselves by following you through life wiping your ass for you at every turn? Don't flatter yourself. If you could make one intelligent decision by yourself we could devote ourselves to worthier pursuits.

ANDREW. Like extramarital affairs.

MARCIA. That's a dangerous topic for you.

ANDREW. What does *that* mean?

IRENE. Why does it have to come to this every time we're together?

OLGA. Because we've learned each other's combat skills to defend ourselves from each other.

IRENE. Why can't we learn something positive from each other? Or is that too radical an idea for this family?

MARCIA. *(to* **IRENE***)* You're right of course, darling. We should learn from your behavior.

ANDREW. *(sheepishly)* And I came here with good news.

OLGA. What, Andrew? Tell us your news.

ANDREW. It's sort of a surprise, really....

*(He opens the manila envelope and extracts three busi-
ness-size envelopes. He distributes one to each of his
sisters.)*

OLGA. What is this?

(The sisters open their envelopes. Each contains a check.)

IRENE. One hundred and seventy-five thousand dollars?

ANDREW. Yes. For each of us.

OLGA. Where did this come from?

ANDREW. From the house in Charleston.

MARCIA. What?

ANDREW. I sold the house in Charleston.

*(The sisters stare incredulously at **ANDREW**. The check
falls from **IRENE**'s hand to the floor.)*

OLGA. You sold the house?

ANDREW. Yes.

OLGA. How could you do that without consulting your sisters?

ANDREW. I'm the executor of the estate.

IRENE. Oh, Andrew.

ANDREW. I'm the executor of the estate. I don't have to
consult you for every decision I make.

MARCIA. No, but I'll bet you consulted your *wife!*

ANDREW. No one wants to be bothered with the details of
maintaining the house, interviewing prospective ten-
ants, collecting the rent. Those responsibilities you
tacitly entrust to me. But when it comes to a decision
of any magnitude –

OLGA. Andrew, listen to yourself.

MARCIA. I suppose you felt you'd made such a success of
that other great decision in your life – your *marriage*
– that you were suddenly qualified to sell our house
without our permission!

ANDREW. I'm a grown man now! I don't have to –

MARCIA. Yes, you do! You don't assume your maturity with thoughtless, inconsiderate acts. That's not manhood –it's *brutishness!*

ANDREW. If I had presented it to you, we would have discussed it endlessly, fought over it, and never reached a decision.

MARCIA. Then that would have been *our choice!*

ANDREW. No. I don't have time for that. I'm starting my family now. I'm not going to be tied to that house and your apron strings for the rest of my life.

MARCIA. Don't throw your Nancyisms in my face. You'll always be tied to us. We're your *sisters!*

(**NANCY** *walks up the terrace steps and strains surreptitiously at the door to see and hear the scene within.*)

OLGA. It's just an excuse, anyway. You did it for the money.

ANDREW. I have my child to think of. That's the future. The house is a thing of the past.

OLGA. Irene and David were planning to move into the house after they were married. Did you know that?

ANDREW. No.

(*to* **IRENE**)

You weren't seriously considering that, were you?

IRENE. When I was in the hospital, remember, we spoke about driving down?

ANDREW. I know, dear, but I thought that was just –

IRENE. The delusions of a sick girl? No, I meant it. And if you were just weaving a sick-bed fantasy for me, I believed it. So completely, it made me stronger, gave me hope for the future. I thought I had one, too, you know – even if it *was* tied to my past.

ANDREW. I'm sorry. I had no idea.

IRENE. Of course not. You've all patted me on the head so many times, you consider it sustenance.

ANDREW. We can still go down.

IRENE. What's there for us now, Andrew? When you sold the house, so much went with it.

(pause)

Father said we should be like one heart beating in four bodies.

(**IRENE** *suddenly turns doubtfully to her sisters*)

Or did he?

(**MARCIA** *and* **OLGA** *share a guilty look.* **IRENE** *laughs to herself.*)

No, of course he didn't.

ANDREW. *(appealing to all three sisters)* The real estate market hasn't been this good in years. I couldn't pass up the opportunity. Seven hundred thousand is a great price.

MARCIA. Yes. A very great price.

(**ANDREW** *crosses and picks up* **IRENE**'s *check from the floor.*)

ANDREW. *(extending the check to* **IRENE***)* Take it, darling. I thought it would make you happy. I thought it would be a wonderful surprise.

(**IRENE** *ignores the check and reaches out and gently touches* **ANDREW**'s *face, almost as if she were saying goodbye to him.*)

IRENE. *(quietly)* No, you didn't.

(**IRENE** *turns away from* **ANDREW**. *He stands motionless in the center of the room as* **NANCY** *enters upstage right.*)

(**NANCY** *stands in the mezzanine and surveys the room. No one responds to her entrance.*)

NANCY. *(to* **ANDREW***)* Did you tell them?

OLGA. He told us.

NANCY. Isn't that good news?

MARCIA. Oh, spare us. He tried that one already.

NANCY. Seven hundred thousand dollars is a great price. The market hasn't been this good in years. Andrew didn't feel he could pass –

MARCIA. *(finishing for her)* – up the opportunity. Yes, we heard the spiel. Let's have our little party and get it over with.

NANCY. You don't have to give me a party. No one's forcing you. Andrew, why don't we just go home.

ANDREW. If you want to.

MARCIA. *(arranging party items on the table)* Nonsense. David is coming, and Dr. Chebrin, and Harry.

NANCY. And Vincent?

MARCIA. No. Vincent won't be here, thank you for asking.

NANCY. *(turning to* **ANDREW***)* Neither will I.

MARCIA. You must. Even though the party isn't for you, anyway. It's for our little unborn nephew, God save him from your genes.

NANCY. Don't talk about my child that way.

MARCIA. He's not a "*child*" yet, dear. Just some protoplasm doing the backstroke in your uterus. Besides, I'm sure he couldn't even hear me.

NANCY. You really hate me, don't you?

MARCIA. No. Not at all. Do you hate a dog for peeing on the carpet? Of course not. She can't help it. It's her nature. You just have to keep her outside.

NANCY. You really hate me.

MARCIA. Is that your goal? Because I just might be able to accommodate you!

OLGA. Stop it, Marcia. You're enjoying this too much.

NANCY. *(to* **ANDREW***)* Are you going to let her talk to me that way?!

ANDREW. Want me to belt her? I don't think it would help

NANCY. I'd like to go.

*(***ANDREW*** crosses woodenly to the stairs.)*

NANCY. *(to all three sisters)* We won't be spending much time together after my child is born.

MARCIA. Don't keep bringing up that child or someone might ask you who the father is.

NANCY. What did you say?

MARCIA. I said, I hear you've been working your way through the school orchestra. Where were you five months ago – the string section? That should narrow it down –

NANCY. *You bitch!*

(NANCY *grabs a heavy glass ashtray from the mezzanine table, hauls back to throw it at* MARCIA, *but* ANDREW *restrains her.*)

MARCIA. No, let her! Let her show her roots!

ANDREW. I'm tempted!

OLGA. Marcia, stop baiting her.

(*The ashtray falls to the floor.* ANDREW *continues to restrain* NANCY.)

ANDREW. *(to* MARCIA*)* Are you happy?!

MARCIA. Are you?!

NANCY. You hypocritical bitch! If you were capable of conceiving you'd be pregnant with that dago's illegitimate bastard!

OLGA. Xenophobia and redundancies all in the same sentence. Go to the back of the class.

(IRENE *sits at the piano and begins playing* – *Brahms's "Valse, Opus 39."*)

(*The upstage left door opens and* HARRY, *carrying refreshments, enters.* DAVID *enters behind him and searches the room for* IRENE.)

HARRY. What's going on?

ANDREW. The usual.

MARCIA. Tell him why, Andrew.

(DAVID quickly descends the left staircase and crosses to IRENE. She barely acknowledges his presence. He stands silently beside her as she continues to play.)

HARRY. This is supposed to be a festive occasion.

MARCIA. It is. And we're all doing what we enjoy most.

HARRY. *(to MARCIA)* I can imagine what that was for you.

ANDREW. She surpassed herself today.

MARCIA. So did you.

NANCY. *(pointing at MARCIA)* That bitch is evil!

HARRY. Olga, why can't you control these situations?

OLGA. *(crossing upstairs)* You'd have to understand the circumstances.

MARCIA. Regardless, Olga, apparently Harry made you class monitor, and you fell short of his expectations.

NANCY. *(to everyone)* I'm leaving. I've tried to be part of this family. I've tried to understand you and be patient with your – Irene, will you stop playing that goddamn thing?!

(IRENE's hands rise from the keyboard, but she does not look up at NANCY.)

I've tried to be patient with your "eccentricities," as Andrew calls them. But I think you're all just low and mean, and not nearly as smart or high class as you think you are – or as I thought you were.

MARCIA. You know, with some assistance from a book of synonyms and antonyms this wouldn't be a bad speech.

NANCY. Shut up! That's just what I mean.

MARCIA. I know. I was helping you illustrate your point.

NANCY. I don't want to be part of your family anymore. I'm starting my own. Andrew, you can decide which one you want to be a part of.

(NANCY exits, slamming the terrace door behind her. She trounces down the steps, then pauses at the base and turns expectantly as:)

(Inside, ANDREW hesitates for a moment.)

MARCIA. The dramatic pause. Go ahead. You made your decision when you gave us *(holding up check)* these.

*(**ANDREW** looks at **MARCIA**, **OLGA**, and **IRENE**, then turns and exits. He closes the terrace door behind him, descends the steps to **NANCY**, who is waiting impatiently. As he approaches her, she lashes out at him:)*

NANCY. Took you long enough to decide to drag your sorry ass out of there!

ANDREW. Jesus, Nancy...

NANCY. Oh, don't Jesus me, Andrew! Just get me a fucking cab!

*(**ANDREW** shakes his head, defeated, as **NANCY** turns contemptuously and exits right. Then, with one final look back at the faculty lounge, **ANDREW** exits the court-yard behind **NANCY**.)*

HARRY. What is that?

MARCIA. Mad money.

HARRY. How appropriate for you.

OLGA. Harry, leave her alone. This isn't the time.

HARRY. Why not? Andrew will be back. He always forgives her.

MARCIA. Assuming I'm the one requiring forgiveness.

DAVID. *(to **IRENE**)* What happened?

IRENE. *(simply)* Vincent left. Andrew sold the house in Charleston.

DAVID. Oh my God.

MARCIA. People in twelve-step programs are so annoyingly honest. It's quite barbaric, really.

HARRY. *(nodding)* I see.

MARCIA. What do you see, you foolish little man.

HARRY. I'm supposed to open my arms to you now –

MARCIA. Please don't bother.

HARRY. As if nothing had happened. I'm supposed to welcome you back –

MARCIA. Is that what you suppose?

HARRY. I'm supposed to welcome you back and forgive you.

MARCIA. Harry, if you want to withhold your approval, intimidate, and give rewards and punishments, buy a dog.

(**DR. CHEBRIN** *enters through the upstage left door and begins crossing down the left staircase.*)

DR. CHEBRIN. Oh, the little mother hasn't arrived yet?

OLGA. The "little mother," as you so appropriately call her, has come and gone.

DR. CHEBRIN. I missed the toast.

OLGA. We all did, Doctor.

DAVID. *(to* **IRENE***)* We don't need the house. We could stay right here in my apartment. And later –

IRENE. Later. It's always later.

DAVID. It'll be alright, Irene. You'll see.

IRENE. Oh, I know sometimes we have to postpone gratification, make concessions. But when we get too far from what we planned for ourselves, when concessions and compromise become our life, we disappear with our aspirations.

DR. CHEBRIN. You're too young to be having such thoughts.

IRENE. Am I, Doctor?

DR. CHEBRIN. Yes. It's all true, of course. But you shouldn't realize it until much later.

OLGA. Your cynicism is discouraging, Doctor.

(**SOKOL** *enters quietly through the upstage left door and stands unnoticed in the mezzanine for a moment.*)

DR. CHEBRIN. I'm not discouraging her. I'm encouraging her to keep her delusions. You need them when you're young.

IRENE. I've had them for so long, I've outgrown them prematurely. And I've sworn off all the substitutes I found. So where does that leave me?

DAVID. You fill the void with love. That's the answer. Everything follows from that.

(**SOKOL** *chuckles slightly.*)

SOKOL. *(mocking)* "You fill the void with love." A convenient philosophy for you to espouse.

DAVID. I wasn't addressing you.

DR. CHEBRIN. *(opening bottle and pouring)* That's our toast. We were going to toast new life. Why not toast love – and hope. They're basically the same thing.

(*Glasses are passed around.*)

(**SOKOL** *removes the book he left on the mezzanine table, turns to exit.*)

DR. CHEBRIN. Mr. Sokol, won't you join us in our toast?

(**SOKOL** *stops, considers.* **DAVID** *eyes him with dread. After a moment,* **SOKOL** *crosses down the left staircase and takes a glass.*)

SOKOL. Certainly. What was it? To love and hope and the Sugar Plum Fairy?

MARCIA. Mr. Sokol, you don't seem to have the esprit de toast. Why don't you just leave us to our comforting ritual.

SOKOL. No. I'd like to join you. Maybe this will be my ticket to Fools Paradise.

DAVID. Why don't you get the hell out of here. Nobody invited you.

IRENE. David...

SOKOL. The sisters did earlier. To toast the expectant mother. Now I see it's shifted to the distraught fiancé.

OLGA. We were just being polite, Mr. Sokol – not realizing the extent of your bitterness and depravity.

SOKOL. Let's toast bitterness – and depravity. They're basically the same thing, right, Doctor?

DR. CHEBRIN. You really should leave, Mr. Sokol.

HARRY. Yes, please do.

*(**SOKOL** pauses for a moment, then quickly swills his drink and slams the glass on the table. He stares intently at **IRENE** for a moment, then turns and strides up the left staircase. **DAVID** walks up the right staircase and stands sentry over **SOKOL**'s exit. **SOKOL** stares insolently at **DAVID** for a moment, then exits through the upstage left door. There is an almost audible sigh of relief from the others as he disappears, leaving the door open behind him.)*

*(**DR. CHEBRIN** lifts his glass:)*

DR. CHEBRIN. To love and hope.

*(Everyone lifts his glass. Suddenly, before glass touches lip, **SOKOL** flies on stage through the open upstage left door and smashes into **DAVID**. To the cries of the others, the two struggle for a moment before **SOKOL** pushes **DAVID** violently, sending them both crashing into the bay window. **IRENE** shrieks as the two fall through the window and vanish into the courtyard below.)*

MARCIA. Oh my God!

*(**HARRY** bounds up the right staircase and rushes through the upstage right door. He crosses the terrace, descends the steps, and disappears into the courtyard behind the lounge. **MARCIA** and **OLGA** shake off their shock and follow him out. **MARCIA** looks down from the terrace as **OLGA** runs down the steps and enters the courtyard. **DR. CHEBRIN** crosses up to the bay window and peers down. **IRENE** stands stationary, in shock, her hands to her face, her eyes still focused on the broken window and the last moment of violence.)*

*(**SOKOL**, stunned, backs into the courtyard right. He stares at the off-stage spot where **DAVID** has fallen.)*

HARRY. *(offstage)* My God, he's not moving!

MARCIA. Harry, his head is bleeding!

OLGA. *(offstage)* He hit the flagstone!

IRENE. Oh my God!

(SOKOL runs up the terrace steps, passes MARCIA, and enters the mezzanine. MARCIA quickly enters behind him. Both she and DR. CHEBRIN watch protectively as:)

(SOKOL, his face a mask of fear and remorse, stands facing IRENE in the main room below. He struggles to speak, but when he sees IRENE shrink in fear from him, he turns away, dashes past DR. CHEBRIN, and exits through the door upstage left.)

MARCIA. Doctor, call the paramedics!

(DR. CHEBRIN rushes to the telephone and dials three digits.)

(IRENE breaks her frozen posture, and MARCIA crosses down the stairs to intercept her.)

DR. CHEBRIN. *(into phone)* Yes, please. A man has fallen and struck his head. He's unconscious.... *(with a glance at IRENE)* Yes, he's bleeding.... Manhattan Crest College, Fifth Avenue at Eighty-seventh. We're in the courtyard behind the faculty lounge.

OLGA. *(offstage)* Check his pulse!

HARRY. *(offstage)* Very faint. Goddamn it, has somebody called a doctor?!

MARCIA. Yes!

(MARCIA meets IRENE on the staircase and prevents her from exiting.)

He'll be alright, darling. Why don't we just wait in here.

IRENE. No, I have to...

(IRENE tries feebly to push past her, but MARCIA restrains her.)

DR. CHEBRIN. *(hanging up receiver)* They'll be here momentarily.

MARCIA. See? Everything's under control.

(MARCIA guides IRENE back into the main room. IRENE no longer resists, but responds docilely as MARCIA leads her to the piano.)

MARCIA. *(soothingly)* Why don't you play something, dear.

(Like a somnambulist, IRENE begins playing Schumann's "Of Foreign Lands and People." She stares numbly into space. MARCIA stands watching her as DR. CHEBRIN exits into the courtyard. With one eye still on IRENE, MARCIA then steals up the stairs to monitor the situation through the bay window.)

(A siren is audible in the distance. As IRENE continues to play, lights dim around her, the offstage sounds grow fainter, and the sounds in IRENE's mind rise as counterpoint to the piano music. Audible in reverb are SOKOL slamming the glass, his angry words with DAVID, sounds of the scuffle between SOKOL and DAVID, cries of shock from the others, as:)

(In real time, sirens grow louder, flashing red lights from offstage bathe the courtyard, and TWO PARAMEDICS carrying a gurney rush into the courtyard right. HARRY and OLGA are visible ushering them to DAVID.)

(In IRENE's mind, the reverbed cries of shock during the struggle continue, then the crash through the window is audible – deafening. Then:)

(Stage lights rise again as the glazed look leaves IRENE's face and a realization and determination take hold. Emerging from her shock, she lifts her hands from the keyboard.)

IRENE. *(quietly)* David...

(then, more lucid, alarmed)

David...!

(**IRENE** *rises and turns away from the piano to face the broken bay window. She then rushes up the right staircase to the door.* **MARCIA** *steps in front of the door to block her exit.*)

MARCIA. Don't. There's nothing you can do.

IRENE. *(assertively)* Stop *protecting* me! Just get out of my way!

(**MARCIA** *hesitates for a moment, then steps aside. As* **IRENE** *exits the upstage right door,* **MARCIA** *turns to stare at the portrait of her father, and:*)

(**IRENE** *runs down the terrace steps as the* **PARAMEDICS**, *flanked by* **HARRY, OLGA,** *and* **DR. CHEBRIN**, *enter the right courtyard with* **DAVID**, *his head braced, his mouth bloodied, on the gurney.*)

IRENE. David!

(**PARAMEDICS** *pause as she rushes to* **DAVID** *'s side and takes his hand.*)

PARAMEDIC ONE. Are you responsible for this man?

IRENE. Yes. He's my husband.

(wiping the blood from **DAVID** *'s face)*

David...?

PARAMEDIC TWO. He has a serious concussion, ma'am. He can't hear you.

IRENE. Yes, he can.

(then, comfortingly)

I'm here, David. I'm with you.

(**MARCIA** *walks out on the terrace and watches as:*)

(**DAVID** *stirs slightly and murmurs.*)

IRENE. He hears me.

(*As* **PARAMEDICS** *exit right with the gurney,* **IRENE** *walks strongly, steadily alongside, holding* **DAVID** *'s hand.* **HARRY** *and* **DR. CHEBRIN** *follow.* **OLGA** *begins to fall in step behind them, but stops and turns to* **MARCIA** *on the terrace landing.*)

(She holds out her hand to **MARCIA**, *who quickly descends the steps and takes her sister's hand.)*

(As piano music rises, the sisters exit right behind the others, and:)

(Curtain falls.)

Set design by Gary Wissman

OTHER TITLES AVAILABLE FROM SAMUEL FRENCH

SIX DANCE LESSONS IN SIX WEEKS

Ricard Alfieri

Comedy / 1m, 1f / Interior

In roles originated by Uta Hagen and David Hyde Pierce, this two-character comedy opens as a aging but still formidable woman hires an acerbic dance instructor to give her lessons in St. Petersburg Beach, Florida. Antagonism between a gay man and the widow of a Southern Baptist minister gives way to profound compatibility as they swing dance, tango, foxtrot and cha-cha while sharing more than dance steps. During the sixth and final lesson, she reveals a closely guarded secret – she is terminally ill – and he shares his greatest gifts-loyalty and compassion. As Michael takes Lily in his arms on the final meeting, they both transcend fear and mortality while the sun sets on their last dance.

THE THREE SISTERS

Anton Chekhov
Adapted by David Mamet based upon a literal
translation by Vlada Chernomordik

Full Length, Drama / 9m, 6f / 2 Ints.,1 Ext.

This poignant story of three provincial sisters who long with all their hearts to go to Moscow is classic theatre which has featured many of the world's great actresses and actors in the roles of Olga, Masha, Irina and Vershinin.